POOR LITTLE RICH GIRL

Elaine discovers that she was adopted at birth; her real mother being Carrie Williams, a best-selling author. She gets Carrie's details from a 'Who's Who' and goes to Cornwall to trace her, but her mother is away. Elaine then takes a job with Carrie's husband, who owns a local antiques shop, and meets Michaela, her young half-sister. However, life becomes complicated when the man she becomes involved with has problems far greater than hers . . .

Books by Phyllis Mallett
in the Linford Romance Library:

LOVE IN PERIL
THE TURNING POINT
LOVE'S MASQUERADE

PHYLLIS MALLETT

POOR LITTLE RICH GIRL

Complete and Unabridged

LINFORD
Leicester

First published in Great Britain in 1988

First Linford Edition
published 2013

A catalogue record for this book is available
from the British Library.

ISBN 978–1–4448–1614–3

Published by
F. A. Thorpe (Publishing)
Anstey, Leicestershire

Set by Words & Graphics Ltd.
Anstey, Leicestershire
Printed and bound in Great Britain by
T. J. International Ltd., Padstow, Cornwall

This book is printed on acid-free paper

1

Elaine Carson sighed as she stepped out of the funeral car and turned to thank the driver. It had been a lonely funeral. Mother had been ill for almost three years and needed constant attention during the last stages of her illness. But now she was laid to rest, and there had been no-one but Elaine to attend and mourn the lonely woman who had lived out her life in this quiet backwater of Essex. Even Shaun had been away on business and unable to attend.

Poor Mother, she thought, sighing again. She looked at the big, sprawling farm house that confronted her, remembered the happy days of her childhood when Father was alive. He had been a cheerful man, larger than life, a farmer who also ran a riding school. Mother had been a more sober person! Staid, almost, but a tower of strength in the lonely years after Father's death.

She felt in her handbag for the front door key. Now Mother was gone she would have to rethink her life. She had run the riding school over the last years, although Mother's illness had caused her to delegate most of the responsibility to her friend Judith. But now there was a void in her life that she had somehow to fill.

The house was pleasantly warm inside, and she repressed a shiver, for outside the cold March wind was blustery and spiteful.

'Would you like a nice cup of tea, dear?' Mrs Kemp's usually cheerful face was set in a respectful frown. The housekeeper had opened the curtain during the time Elaine was at the funeral and now the house seemed normal once again.

'Yes, please.' Elaine moved towards the lounge, but paused when she heard the sound of a car drawing up outside. Shaun? Her heart was heavy. She needed company at a time like this!

Even Shaun would be better than no-one! She turned and hurried back to the door, opened it hopefully. But it wasn't Shaun, and her lips became compressed as she watched the tall figure of William Morley, the family solicitor, coming up the garden path.

'Good afternoon, Elaine!' He paused to raise his hat. In late middle-age, he was quite old as far as Elaine was concerned, for at 23 she felt that anyone over 35 was ancient, and Morley was probably the wrong side of 50. 'I hope I'm not too early,' he continued. 'I had other business in the area, and thought I could wait if you had not completed your family obliga-tions.'

'That's all right, Mr Morley.' She opened the door wider. 'Please come in. It's good of you to call so soon after the funeral.'

He eyed her critically as he crossed the threshold, removing his hat and clutching his briefcase. Despite the pallor in her cheeks she was a beautiful girl, he noted. Tall and slender, she had naturally wavy chestnut hair and eyes that were so dark brown they sometimes appeared black.

'My business won't keep you long.' He spoke in a kindly tone as Mrs Kemp bustled foward to take his hat and coat.

'We'll go into the lounge,' she decided. 'Would you please bring us some tea. Mrs Kemp?'

'I put the kettle on the minute I heard you returning,' the housekeeper replied. 'There'll be tea in a few moments.'

Elaine led the way into the lounge and motioned Morley to a seat. But he moved to the window and peered out at the lawn and garden.

'I shall miss seeing this particular view,' he said softly as he went on to take a seat before the fire burning in the big grate. 'I've been coming here for more than thirty years, and this, I fancy, will be the last time.'

'Won't you act as my solicitor?' she demanded, frowning as she studied him. 'You've been handling Carson family business for longer than I can remember.'

'I would welcome the opportunity to serve you as I served Mr and Mrs Carson!' He nodded, thrusting his hands toward the leaping flames in the grate. 'But I fancy that you will sell up here and go to the city. I always got the impression that you took after your mother. By all accounts, she loved the bright lights.'

'Mother?' Elaine frowned as she gazed at him. 'What on earth are you talking about, Mr Morley? I could never persuade Mother to visit London unless it was for a very special reason, and when Father was alive he always had the greatest difficulty in getting her to make the trip. She hated the bright lights!'

'You're talking of Mrs Carson, aren't you?' he asked.

'Of course! Who were you talking about?' Elaine looked perplexed.

The silence pounded again, and

dragged on for several moments, deepening ominously.

'I have a nasty suspicion that you haven't been told,' he said, at length.

'Told what?' It was Elaine's turn to frown as she leaned forward in her seat and fixed him with a keen gaze. 'Are you talking in riddles, Mr Morley, or am I finally going mad? It was bound to happen, I should think, after the events of the past weeks.'

'I'm sorry, Elaine.' His face betrayed concern. 'It's obvious that you don't know! And I thought they had told you years ago!' He shook his head. 'This isn't the best time for such a revelation. Perhaps we could talk about it at a later date?'

'You must tell me now! I wouldn't be able to sleep a wink until I saw you again.'

'Mr and Mrs Carson were not your natural parents.' His voice was low-pitched.

'Not my natural parents!' she echoed. 'What do you mean?'

'They adopted you at birth.' He exhaled deeply. 'I'm sorry to break this to you at this particular time, Elaine.'

Elaine slumped in her chair with shock, her mind thrust up a rapid succession of images from the past. 'Then who were my real parents? Do you know?'

'Your father was killed in a road accident before you were born, and your real mother never saw you, I understand. You were taken from her at birth, adopted by Mr and Mrs Carson. Really, Elaine, I think you should have been told much sooner.'

'I can't believe this!' she said, shaking her head. 'It's like some horrible nightmare.' She drew a deep breath and fought for control, making a supreme effort to appear calm. 'If you know so much about my past then tell me who my real mother is.'

Morley sighed. 'It's a difficult situation,' he hedged. 'I expect your mother has made another life for herself. If you suddenly turned up on her doorstep there could be complications.'

'I haven't the slightest intention of barging in on her,' Elaine protested.

'Shall we get down to the business in hand?' he countered, fumbling with the briefcase. 'I came to inform you of the contents of Mrs Carson's will, as she charged me to do immediately after her funeral.'

'Despite the mystery of my origins,' Elaine said firmly, 'I shall always look upon her as my mother, which she was, to all intents and purposes. My real mother, whoever she is, could not have treated me better.'

'I'm well aware of that!' Morley nodded his agreement. 'Thank goodness you have a great deal of commonsense, Elaine. That's why I thought you had been told about the adoption. The Carsons ought to have confided in you.'

'The adoption itself is nothing to worry about,' Elaine responded. 'I can get used to the idea. But I would like to know about my real parents. Were they from this part of the country?'

'Your father was in the city with a firm of stock-brokers. At the time of your birth your mother was a journalist on one of the large London dailies.'

'And my father was killed in a road accident?'

'Yes. About three weeks before you were born!'

'That was terrible! My mother! How on earth did she manage to survive that?'

'Evidently she could not handle the death of your father and your arrival, so you were put up for adoption.'

'Do you know who she is?' Elaine leaned forward in her chair, but Mrs Kemp entered the room at that moment with a tray, and she lapsed into silence until after the housekeeper had departed.

Morley sipped his tea reflectively, his gaze expressing concern as he looked at Elaine over the rim of his cup. Then he leaned back in his seat and tried to relax.

'Carrie Williams,' Morley said. 'Have

you heard of her?'

Elaine frowned as she considered, and then shook her head. 'The name is familiar but I can't place it. Is she my mother?'

'Yes. And these days she's a best-selling author.'

'That Carrie Williams!' Elaine caught her breath. 'Of course! I've read some of her books! And she's my mother?'

'I believe so!' Morley waved his papers impatiently. 'Now, if I could have your attention for a few moments we can settle this business.'

Elaine opened her mouth to protest but he was adamant, and she fought down her sudden excitement as he read the will.

There were several bequests to charities, as Elaine had expected. But everything remaining of the Carson estate had been left to her, and she was amazed by the size of the inheritance. The farm and riding school were hers, as were two smaller farms in the district, and there was a sizeable fortune in two bank accounts.

Elaine was stunned. She'd had no idea of the extent of the family's wealth.

'I can see that you are somewhat overwhelmed by all of this,' Morley said in a kindly tone. 'You have so much to attend to now, Elaine. But you will need to keep your mind occupied during this difficult time. If there is anything I can do to help then you have only to pick up the nearest telephone. The business practically runs itself, so admirably did both Mr and Mrs Carson manage their affairs. There will be some papers for your signature in due course, but everything is straightforward and you have nothing to worry about. Now all that remains is for me to wish you luck.'

'Thank you for being so helpful,' she said as she saw him to the door.

He nodded and departed, and Elaine felt overwhelmed by loneliness as she closed the door after him. But then a car horn sounded outside, and she opened the door again to see Shaun's saloon coming into the yard. Some of the tension left her at the sight of his grinning face as he sprang out of the car. Mr Morley was driving out of the yard, and Shaun paused and turned to stare after him before coming to where Elaine stood.

He was tall and dark, with glinting brown eyes and an easy smile. He was a rep for motorists' accessories, and worked the south-east of England for a large company.

'Hello, Elaine!' He paused on the doorstep and held out his arms to her, his face assuming a woebegone expression. 'I'm so sorry I couldn't get back for the funeral. But I thought of you. It must have been terrible, handling it all alone.'

'It's over now, Shaun,' she said quietly, taking hold of his hands. 'And I'm glad you're here! I've been so lonely.'

'You'd never be lonely again if you'd marry me,' he retorted. 'Wasn't that Morley, the lawyer, who was leaving?'

'Yes. He came to tell me what was in

12

Mother's will.' Elaine almost stumbled over the word 'Mother'. Mrs Carson was the only mother she had ever known, and yet she had a natural mother somewhere out there in the world. 'Come in, Shaun.'

'There's something I have to tell you,' she said slowly when they were sitting at the roaring fire. 'And I can hardly believe it myself.'

'What? Have the Carsons more money and property put by somewhere else?'

'No.' Elaine shook her head, irritated by his attempts at lightness. 'Mr Morley told me that they were not my real parents. They adopted me when I was born.'

Shaun's face mirrored his amazement, and for a moment he stared silently at her. Then he moistened his lips.

'Because you're not their real child, there's no danger that you'll not get the estate, is there?' he demanded, and she saw worry in his keen eyes. He sighed.

'Did he tell you anything about your real parents?' he went on. Then he paused and shook his head.

'Elaine! My dear girl! What a time you've had of it! Look, I've got a couple of weeks holiday due to me shortly. Why don't we pack up and depart for places unknown? I'm sure you're going to need more than a fortnight, but I am only a working man, and that's the best I can offer at the moment.'

She studied him, not really liking what she fancied were the undercurrents of his mind. Her opinion of him had been confirmed — he had only stayed around because of her expected inheritance.

'The first thing I want to do is locate my real mother and see what she looks like.' She spoke slowly, but there was determination in her tone. 'It's strange that I've found out about her at this particular time, when I'm lonely and depressed.'

'You're not thinking of confronting her, are you?'

'I'm not thinking anything in particular at the moment,' she replied. 'But I wouldn't do anything stupid, Shaun! If I found out where she is living I'd do no more than write to her and go to see her only if she agreed. She'll be in her middle forties now, I expect. That means she is probably married again and has a family growing up.'

She paused and smiled as the possibilities came to her. 'I may have sisters and brothers! What a marvellous thought!' She clasped her hands. 'But perhaps she hasn't told anyone about me, and I could be quite an embarrassment for her, turning up out of the blue.'

'Do you have anything to go on? Did Morley tell you anything about her?'

'Yes!' Elaine caught her breath. 'She's quite famous! I'd really like to see her! But only from a distance, unless — ' She broke off and sat down by the window to stare out at the distant countryside. 'I thought I was all alone in the world,' she whispered. 'I came back from the funeral completely alone. It's a dreadful feeling, knowing there's no family of any kind waiting for you.' She threw a reproachful glance at him. 'Even you weren't here, Shaun! I do think you could have made an effort to be with me today!'

'I thought I had explained all that!' He shook his head. 'I've been working to the limit because some of the sales staff are off sick. I would have been here with you if it had been at all possible! But you don't have to worry now! I'm here and I'll take time off if you really need my company.'

'What's suddenly so different?' she queried. 'Before the funeral there was nothing you could do to be with me. Work came first! But now the funeral is over and I've got my inheritance you suddenly find that you could get some time off if I really need you! Well, at the moment I don't know what I want, so there would be no point in you taking a holiday.'

'Whatever you do, I'm going to see that you don't sit moping in this big house.' He spoke firmly. 'I think you'd better come home with me! Mother said to ask you to visit. It isn't good for you to be alone right now.'

'That's kind of your mother but I'm staying here until I can get myself sorted out. There's so much to think about and do! And I have some inquiries to make!' A sudden decision came to her and she arose quickly. 'It was good of you to come Shaun, but you'll have to excuse me now. There's something I must do.'

'I'll wait until you've finished,' he protested. 'I'm going to take you out later. You're not to bury yourself in this house.'

'That's the last thing I shall do.' She shook her head. 'I've got the business to take care of and the riding school to run. And I need to be on my own right now to think things over. Goodbye, Shaun. Call me sometime tomorrow, will you?'

He arose with another protest on his lips, but she was firm, and there was a tight little smile upon her lips when she closed the door behind him as he left . . .

2

Elaine's heart thudded with excitement as she sat down at the telephone and dialled the local lending library. She recognised the woman's voice that answered, and moistened her lips.

'Hello, Sue, it's Elaine,' she said.

'Elaine! How did the funeral go?'

'Quite uneventful.' Elaine shook her head sadly. 'It's all over now.' She paused. 'Sue, I've read several books by the author Carrie Williams.'

'Who hasn't?' Sue cut in. 'Do you want her latest reserved?'

'I'd like to find out something about the author herself.' Elaine had to fight to make her voice sound natural. 'How would I go about it?'

'There are several 'Who's Who' books on the market. Hang up and I'll check what we have in stock and then call you back. By the way, exactly what do you want to know?'

'What sort of thing do they list about authors?'

'The usual stuff. Name, address, marital status, offspring and literary achievements, usually in that order. Will that do?'

'Perfectly, if you have it on hand.' Elaine crossed her fingers. 'Call me back as soon as you can, Sue.'

'Leave it to me.' The line went dead, and Elaine hung up with trembling fingers.

The door was opened and Mrs Kemp looked in.

'Elaine, Judith is here. Shall I bring her in or tell her you'll see her tomorrow?'

'Tomorrow?' Elaine frowned.

'I was thinking that you wouldn't want to be bothered with business today.'

'It doesn't matter. Please show her in.' Elaine went to sit at the telephone desk, fingers tapping impatiently as she waited for the phone to ring. She could hear Mrs Kemp's voice in the hall, and Judith made some reply before appearing in the doorway, where she paused to gaze critically at Elaine.

'Hello, Judith. Come in and close the door. Is something wrong?'

'No. I was wondering about you, that's all. I guessed you would be back from the funeral by now, and I didn't like to think of you being here alone in the house.'

'That was thoughtful of you, but I'm all right.' She glanced at the telephone, hoping that it wouldn't ring until after Judith had left.

'Would you like me to stay with you tonight?' Judith asked.

'I don't know if I shall be here tonight,' Elaine replied. 'I'm waiting for a telephone call, and if I get the information I'm hoping for I may leave very shortly.'

'That sounds interesting.' Judith Allen was a tall blonde with a quiet manner. She and Elaine had been friends from childhood. Judith lived on a neighbouring farm, and she and Elaine shared an undying love for horses.

'I can't tell you about it right now, Judith.' Elaine tried to soften her tone a little. 'You know I'm very grateful for the way you have rallied round.'

'Think nothing of it. What are friends for?' Judith smiled.

'We've got to have a chat about the future.' Elaine shrugged. 'So much is happening now. I've seen Mr Morley. He told me that I've inherited everything here, which means I now own the riding school, among other things. If I go away for a time, will you be able to cope alone, Judith?'

'Yes. There are no worries about that! A number of girls would love to come and help out around the place. Then there's Nick. He's finished agricultural college now. He's worth his weight in gold.'

'Why don't you get him to the altar and make certain of him?' Elaine teased.

Judith shook her head. 'It's not me dragging my feet,' she protested. 'Nick wants to be on his own farm before he takes a wife.'

'He's doing very well managing this place.' Elaine was suddenly thoughtful.

'But this is only temporary!' Judith sighed. 'He knows you will be taking over when everything is settled.'

'Perhaps I won't.' Elaine shook her head. 'If Nick became the tenant here, would that help your situation?'

'You can't mean that!' Judith's eyes gleamed. 'Are you pulling my leg?'

Elaine smiled. 'Give me a day or two to collect myself,' she said, 'and then we'll go into details. But, in the meantime, find out what Nick's thoughts are about becoming the tenant here.' She paused and frowned. 'Would you still want to run the riding school if you married Nick?'

'If we were living here I'd love to keep it going.' Judith nodded. 'It would be the chance of a lifetime, Elaine.'

'Let's leave it like that then. Right

23

now my mind is on another matter, and until I've got it sorted out I shan't be able to rest.'

'Is it anything I can help with?' Judith was immediately concerned.

'If I do need any help then you can rest assured that you'll be the first person I'll turn to,' Elaine promised.

'Then I'll get back to work.' Judith opened the door. She smiled as she glanced back over her shoulder. 'You've made my day, Elaine!'

The telephone rang as Judith departed, and Elaine paused for a moment before lifting the receiver. Her heart thudded when she heard Sue's voice.

'Hello, Elaine. Sorry I took a little time. But I have the details of Carrie Williams right here. Do you want to write them down?'

'Yes, please, Sue. Just a moment.' Elaine pulled a pad from a drawer and picked up a pen. 'Right. Fire away!' she began to write as Sue gave her the details.

'Carrie Williams,' Sue said slowly, 'Born January eight, nineteen-forty in Chelmsford, Essex, England; daughter of Arthur (a civil engineer) and Helen (Rix) Yelding; married Frank Templeton, antique dealer, June twenty-fourth, nineteen sixty-five; children: Lorna Ann, Paul Richard, Michaela. Home address, The Cliff House, Goonstell Road, St Ann's Bay, Cornwall.'

'Is that it?' Elaine demanded when Sue lapsed into silence.

'That's all of the personal details. You can have a list of her books if you wish.'

'Not right now. Thank you, Sue. It's a great help. I'll be in touch later.'

'Anything else I can do for you?' Sue offered.

'No, honestly. Everything is all right.'

'Goodbye then. See you soon.'

' 'Bye,' Elaine responded, and hung up.

She leaned back in her seat and stared at the notes she had made. There was the address where her mother was living. She had married Frank Templeton. But where was St Ann's Bay in Cornwall?

She hurried out to her car and picked up a road map. Smoothing it out on the bonnet of the car, she studied Cornwall, and soon found St Ann's Bay to the west of Looe. Her heartbeats quickened as she stared at the spot. Her only relative was living there!

But what happened now? She needed to ask someone's advice and there was only Shaun! She felt guilty when she thought of him for she was not in love with him! For a long time she suspected that any love she'd had for him in the first place had disappeared. He was away a great deal in his job and she had found nursing Mrs Carson a full-time job towards the end.

And Shaun had gotten into the habit of spending her expected inheritance on grandiose schemes. She could imagine the kind of life she would have if she married him! And she could not discuss her future with him. He would only try to talk her out of meeting her natural mother, and then propose again. He would not understand that marriage was the last thing she needed at this time!

She stifled a sigh. What was happening to her emotions? She was drying out, like an arid field.

Impulsively, she summoned Mrs Kemp and bade the housekeeper sit down. There was a solemn expression on the woman's face, as if she expected to be told that her employment would be ended. But Elaine drew a deep breath and launched herself into the topic that now occupied her attention.

'Mrs Kemp, did you know that I was adopted as a baby?' she demanded.

'You? Adopted?' Mrs Kemp shook her head. 'I never knew that! I thought you was their own! There was never anything to suggest you weren't.'

'No, of course not!' Elaine shook her head. 'Well, that's short and sweet. If you had known about it I could have asked you some questions, but as you're as much in the dark as I then you can't help,' Elaine said flatly.

'I'm sorry, dear. I wish there was something I could do. It must have been a shock for you, learning about that on top of the funeral! Did the lawyer tell you?'

'Yes! It was a big shock! It means that I have a natural mother out there, and probably some brothers and sisters too.'

'Don't you have any idea who your real mother is?'

'I'm making inquiries, and that's really why I've called you. I may be going away for a few days! While I'm away you can carry on as before. But I expect there will be some changes when I get organised and see what's to be done.'

'Does that mean my job may be coming to an end?' Mrs Kemp demanded.

'I really don't know at the moment! I'm sorry I can't be more definite. I suppose it really depends on what I find out about my real mother. But don't take that as meaning I'll be dispensing with your services. I have to go on living here because of the business, and I certainly won't be able to run this house and do all the other work. I won't even have the time to run the riding school.'

'Judith sounded eager to handle that!' Mrs Kemp got to her feet. 'Don't worry about me, Elaine. I've been the housekeeper here for twenty years. I'll just carry on until you can make up your mind.'

'Thank you, Mrs Kemp.' Elaine felt easier as the housekeeper departed. 'And don't get alarmed if you don't see me around for a few days,' she called.

She tried to relax when she was alone, but found it impossible. She knew she couldn't settle to her new way of life until she had met the unknown woman who had borne her.

The decision came suddenly, and the moment she was resolved upon it she picked up the telephone and called Shaun's number. Mrs Appleby answered, and broke into a torrent of condolences when she recognised Elaine's voice. Eventually, Shaun came to the phone.

'Hello! Feeling better now?' he demanded.

'I've called to tell you that I'll be leaving home for a few days, Shaun,' she began.

He interrupted her with a shout of surprise. 'Where are you going, for heaven's sake?'

'I have to make some inquiries, that's all, and I can't do it from home.'

'Where are you going?' he repeated.

'I don't know exactly!' She shrugged. 'I'll phone you when I get there.'

'That's not good enough, Elaine! You can't go off just like that! Anything could happen to you.'

'Please listen,' she cut in. 'My mind is made up! I am going away tomorrow! And I don't know how long I shall be gone. I'll call you if you're going to be worried about me!'

'Let me take some time off work and

go with you,' he pleaded.

'No! I have to do this myself. I need to be alone for a time.'

'Can't you give me some idea where you'll be?' he asked desperately.

'Cornwall.' She smiled wryly. 'That's as near as I can tell you. Now I must say goodbye. I've got some packing to do, and I need an early night. I'll be on the road before seven tomorrow. I'll be in touch as soon as I can.'

'Don't hang up yet!' he commanded. 'Listen! I love you! I'll be waiting when you get back!'

'Goodbye!' She hung up, and breathed deeply until a pulse fluttered in her throat. Her heart was pounding madly. She felt as if she were standing at a crossroads in her life. For too long she had been tied down by family duty. Now she was free, like a bird released from a cage, and she needed to take flight, to test her wings, so to speak, and have a real taste of freedom!

3

When she set out early the next morning, Elaine could hardly believe that she was actually on the way to find her real mother! She drove steadily, filled with a sense of adventure. She had never been to Cornwall before, but a few minutes with a road map the night before had enabled her to work out a route that would get her to her distant destination.

She by-passed London and settled down on the A30. Time passed as if it did not exist. It had been more than two years since her last holiday, and her mother's illness had kept her tied at the farm 24 hours a day. Now she experienced the intangible grip of freedom, and luxuriated in it.

It was early afternoon when she crossed the Tamar bridge into Cornwall, and she pulled off the road to check her map. Going on, she watched the road signs, and eventually reached the coast. She pulled off the road overlooking St Ann's Bay and sat gazing down at the grey sea. Cliffs reared up from sea level, and there were ships far out, indistinct and anonymous, which was exactly how she felt. She followed the line of the bay with her eyes and saw a town in the distance. Checking her map again, she realised that the town was Goonstell, and decided to go there before making any inquiries.

She had never encountered such hills before, and drove very carefully, thankful that the summer season had not yet commenced, which meant that the traffic was light. Goonstell itself was a maze of inclines and declines. There was a tall church on a hill, and slag heaps on the skyline in the distance, looking like small pyramids. She left the car in a multi-storey car park and checked the details that had been gleaned about her mother from the library.

Frank Templeton, she mused. Her mother's second husband. She knew he dealt in antiques. Perhaps he had a shop in the area? She found a telephone box and leafed through the yellow pages, and a thrill stabbed through her when she found the name and the business. Falmouth Road! She walked around the little streets until she found it, and then stood looking in the window of the shop while her thoughts flowed thick and fast.

There was a biggish man inside the shop, tall and heavy, with a beard and a shock of brown hair. He was wearing a pair of grey flannels and a tweed sports jacket. She guessed that he was Frank Templeton, and he glanced at her through the window. The shop was otherwise deserted.

There was a card in the window advertising a vacancy for a seasonal shop assistant. Elaine was seized by an impulse to talk to this man who had married her mother, and entered the shop and walked to the far end, her nerve almost failing as he looked up.

'Can I help you?' He had a friendly voice, cultured and warm.

'I — er, I've come about the vacancy,' she said quickly. 'I want to stay in Cornwall for the summer, and I'll need a job to be able to do that.'

'I see!' Brown eyes surveyed her intently. 'Have you had shop experience? Do you know anything about antiques?'

'No.' She shook her head, hardly aware of what she was saying. 'I nursed my mother for the last two years. Her funeral was yesterday. I just couldn't stay at home any longer so I came to Cornwall.'

'I'm sorry about your mother. My name is Templeton — Frank Templeton.'

Elaine was casting around in her mind for something else to say. She had a feeling that she was handling this very badly. He had such intense eyes! They seemed to bore right through her. Then she spotted a Carrie Williams book on

35

his desk and an inaudible sigh escaped her.

'Are you reading that?' she asked.

He glanced down at the book and a smile touched the corners of his mouth. 'I read all my wife's books,' he said softly.

'Your wife? You're married to Carrie Williams!'

'I am most certainly! Have you read her stories?'

'Most of them.' She nodded. 'Well, that's amazing! I didn't know she lived in Cornwall!'

'She has to live somewhere! And a lot of writers choose Cornwall. There's something in the scenery and the atmosphere that's good for them.' He smiled and picked up the book, turned it over, and Elaine's heart gave a sudden lurch, for there was a photograph of her mother on the back.

'May I see that? she asked, and her lips twisted spasmodically as a shaft of pure emotion stabbed through her.

'Certainly!' He smiled and handed

over the book, her reaction exactly what he had expected. Although he had no way of knowing the truth.

Elaine stared at the face of the woman who had borne her and saw something of her own features mirrored in the countenance that stared at her. She suppressed a gasp and looked up at Frank Templeton, half expecting him to comment upon the resemblance. But he merely smiled.

'You seem quite taken by my wife,' he remarked. 'If you work here you'll see her often. But at the moment she is away on business. I'm not expecting her back for another three weeks.'

'I see! You must think me a complete idiot, but I've read most of her books, and I've never seen an author in the flesh before.'

'They're just like other people!' He chuckled. 'Well, perhaps not! But don't quote me on that! Least of all to my wife! Now what about you filling the vacancy I have? You say you've had no shop experience, and you know nothing about antiques?'

'That's right.' She nodded, crest-fallen. If her mother was not returning for three weeks then she needed to fill in the time while waiting.

'I suppose that could be an advantage,' he mused. 'I sometimes think that the less one knows about this business the better. So I can't hold your inexperience against you. What I am really looking for is reliability! The stock I hold here is worth many thousands of pounds! So I must be able to trust whoever I employ! More than that, I need someone who will stay right through the summer. When the holiday season starts in a few weeks it will be hectic until October.'

'I'd certainly stay right through the season,' she said.

'What sort of work have you been doing, apart from nursing your mother?'

'I ran a riding school.' She moistened her lips. 'My father was a farmer. He had three farms and the riding school. When he died, Mother took over, and now she's dead!'

'And you walked out this morning!' He eyed her keenly.

'I've left staff in charge.' She shrugged.

'But can you stay away for the entire summer?'

'Yes. My friend Judith runs the riding school. Her future husband has been running the farm for months. He graduated from agricultural college last autumn. I'm hoping he'll step into the farm as a tenant.'

'And the other two farms?'

'They have tenants. I shan't be missed, and I need to keep away to give my mind a rest.'

'Well . . . ' He pondered. 'Obviously, what you lack in shop experience you make up for with business sense. Shall I give you two weeks trial to see how you fit in? It may be that you won't like the job, and if you leave at the end of two weeks I'll still have time to get someone permanent for the summer.'

'Thank you. I'd like a chance. And I

won't leave. I'm sure you'll find me suitable.'

'There's not much to the job really,' he admitted. 'I have to leave the place quite frequently, and you'd merely stand in for me while I'm away. Apart from that, you'll dust the objects and run things generally. Would you like to make a start tomorrow morning, if that's convenient for you?'

'Yes, please!' she nodded excitedly.

'Then you'd better tell me your name!' He smiled.

'Elaine Carson. I live near Billericay in Essex.'

'And where are you planning to stay while you're in Cornwall?'

'I haven't given that a thought,' she admitted. 'I don't really mind. Perhaps I can book into a hotel for the present. But that's just a detail.'

The shop door was thrust open at that moment and the bell rang shrilly. Elaine looked over her shoulder to see a schoolgirl, aged about 10, entering. She gasped in horror as the child almost collided with a statuette and set it rocking. The girl paused, grasped the piece of sculpture and steadied it.

'Daddy!' She came forward again, catching her hip against a small table and setting the glass ornaments upon it trembling and tottering.

'Michaela, please don't get so excited! I've told you many times not to come into the shop if you're going to behave like a runaway bull!'

'Why haven't you gone home?' Frank demanded, grimacing at Elaine.

'Lee asked me to go riding. As I didn't go on Sunday I thought I'd make up for it now.' Michaela was looking at Elaine as she spoke, who smiled at her.

'Here's someone who could probably teach you a thing or two about riding,' Frank introduced. 'This is Elaine Carson, Michaela, and she's coming to work in the shop this summer. She owns a riding school in Essex.'

'Then why does she want to work in your shop all summer?' Michaela demanded.

'You'll have to excuse Michaela,' Frank said to Elaine. 'She becomes a real handful whenever her mother is away on business. The rest of the time I don't know she's around, and she never comes into the shop, which is a blessing when you take into account the way she just entered.'

'I miss Mother,' Michaela said. Her face was grave. 'I wish she didn't have to go away so often. I'm the only one at school whose mother keeps going away.' She turned her attention to Elaine. 'Do you have a horse of your own?' she asked.

'I own fifteen,' Elaine admitted. 'But there is one who's rather special. I always have to carry a piece of sugar for her, and if I forget then she won't let me ride her.'

'I have a pony! I keep it at Lee's riding school! Lee's father owns the school! My mother has a mare there. She's a beauty! I want a horse like Juno when I grow up! I'll bet you can ride well, can't you?'

'Fairly well!' Elaine nodded.

'I'm sorry to break in on this,' Frank said gently. 'But Elaine hasn't anywhere to stay at the moment. I know of a suitable hotel, Elaine, and I'll give them a ring. Michaela could take you there. You'll soon get used to Goonstell, but you could get lost until you become familiar with it.'

'I've got Lee outside with his Aunt Margaret,' Michaela protested. 'I have to be going.'

'It's all right,' Elaine hastened to say. 'I'll be able to manage all right.'

'You'll have to come out to Lee's place,' Michaela said, turning to the door and almost colliding with another table of ornaments. 'I'll tell Lee about you, and you'll be able to come with me when you get a half day.'

'Thanks.' Elaine smiled. 'I was hoping that I'd get the chance to do some riding this summer.'

'Goodbye now,' Michaela responded, and dashed from the shop.

'Michaela will be a friend for life if

you talk horses to her,' Frank remarked. 'She's a good girl, but she does miss her mother at times like these.' He went to straighten an ornament that had almost fallen from the display table, then glanced at his watch. 'It's almost closing time,' he mused. 'If you could wait ten minutes I'll be able to see that you get settled somwhere comfortable. But it's going to cost you a great deal to live in a hotel all summer.'

'I don't have to worry about money,' Elaine declared. 'I need the job as something to occupy my mind rather than the means of making a living.'

'Make yourself at home then. If you'd rather not be left on your own on your first evening in a strange place then I'll be happy to take you home with me. You could have dinner with us — us being myself, Michaela and my eldest daughter Lorna. My son, Paul, is at Cambridge.'

'You're very kind! Thank you for the invitation. But I am rather tired, and I have a splitting headache. I think I'll just book into a hotel and have a quiet evening.'

'Certainly. I understand how you must be feeling. But permit me to see you to the hotel. It's just around the corner.'

When he closed the shop, Frank accompanied Elaine to her car to collect her luggage, and then took her to a small residential hotel overlooking the church. When he finally departed, Elaine sank down thankfully upon the bed in her room and closed her eyes. The excitement and tensions of the day had really given her a headache.

But after taking a shower and changing her clothes, she felt more relaxed, and went down to the dining room for a meal. By the time she had eaten her headache was abating, and she was drinking coffee when a tall, dark-haired man entered the dining room and paused to look over the diners. There were four other diners present, and he soon dismissed them. Gazing at Elaine, he began to approach,

45

and she frowned for she did not know him.

'Excuse me!' He smiled hesitantly. 'Miss Carson?'

'Yes. I'm Elaine Carson.'

'Please forgive my intrusion! Frank Templeton said you were tired from travelling, but I just had to come and see you!'

'Really!' She frowned. He was handsome, she decided, although his face showed tension and his eyes seemed too intent. His manner suggested that he was here under protest, but that the business on his mind was very important to him.

'May I sit down?' He placed a hand on the back of a chair opposite. 'I won't take up more than a few minutes of your time.'

She nodded and he pulled out the chair and sat down, then leaned an arm on the table and gazed at her.

'This must seem like the most appalling cheek,' he went on. 'But permit me to introduce myself. I'm

Adrian Curtis. I own the local riding school.'

'Ah!' A light showed at the end of the tunnel in Elaine's mind.

He smiled. 'Michaela, Frank's daughter, was singing your praises to my son, Lee, and I gathered that you know all about horses and are keen to work in this area for the entire summer. Well, I'm on the point of closing down because I can't get the right people to help me, and I was wondering if you would prefer to work with horses instead of in a shop?' He paused and waited for her initial reaction.

'Oh!' Elaine drew a deep breath. 'I don't know what to think, Mr Curtis. I've just arranged to work a two-week trial with Mr Templeton. I'm due to start work with him tomorrow.'

'I've had a chat with Frank and he's willing to have you work for him mornings only, if you'd care to come to the riding school in the afternoons!'

Elaine raised an eyebrow and he nodded, smiling wryly.

'It's all been happening behind the scenes, hasn't it? And I wouldn't blame you if you turned me down. It probably doesn't sound right anyway, a perfect stranger trying to arrange your life to suit his needs! But it's not like that really! When I heard Michaela talking it seemed that someone up there had heard my prayers at last.'

He paused, watched her face for a moment, and then said, 'But your expression indicates a refusal!' He pushed back the chair and started to rise. 'I'm sorry I bothered you, Miss Carson! You'd probably be better off in an antique shop anyway!'

'I haven't said I wouldn't consider working for you,' she countered. 'But I would like some time in which to think it over, if you don't mind.'

'Certainly!' He grinned, and his whole face seemed to discard worry and age. His expression became hopeful as he sat down again. 'Perhaps I ought to tell you something about myself and the riding school.'

'I'd like to hear it,' she responded.

'It was my wife's school, really!' A bitter light suddenly gleamed in his dark eyes. 'I'm an artist, or I was until Sylvia had a fall from a horse and died after lying in a coma for two months!' He exhaled sharply and shook his head. 'That was almost three years ago! I gave up my career to manage the riding school, temporarily in the first place, and to be with my son.' He paused, shaking his head sadly. 'But the place has slowly been going down hill! My heart is not in it! Lee is eight now, and when he's old enough to face a complete break I'll probably move right away from Cornwall. But that's in the future. Right now I have to keep the business going, and try to improve it if I can! But I need some expert help!' He sighed. 'If I don't get it soon then nothing can save me from defeat.'

Elaine exhaled slowly. He seemed to be the kind of man who would not accept defeat gracefully. She could imagine him fighting tooth and nail to achieve his aims.

'That's about all there is to tell!' He gave a bitter laugh. 'Not much to show for the years of work that's been put into the place, not to mention the life of my wife.'

'If I can help then I'm sure we can come to some agreement,' Elaine said tentatively. 'One thing I do know about is horses! I own a riding school in Essex.'

'So Michaela informed me.' He smiled. 'She was insistent that I come to see you! Her enthusiasm infected my son, so here I am!'

'Perhaps I could have a look around your place,' she suggested. 'If Mr Templeton is prepared to employ me on a part-time basis then I'd like to work with horses this summer. I miss my own horse already!'

'Fine!' He leaned forward, his expression softening again. 'Are you doing anything this evening, or are you too tired after your trip?'

'I had a headache earlier but that

seems to have cleared up. I have nothing to occupy my time this evening, so we could get some of the preliminaries out of the way if you wish.'

'Certainly. I have my car outside. I'll drive you out to my place.'

Elaine immediately picked up her handbag and they departed. He led her to his car and settled her in the front passenger seat. She studied him as he went around the car to get in behind the wheel. He was in his late 20s, she judged, and seemed a genuine type. They were silent until the town was behind them, and then Elaine moistened her lips.

'I expect you're wondering what I'm doing contemplating a summer in Cornwall when I have a business back in Essex.' She spoke a trifle harshly.

He shook his head. 'That's your business,' he replied. 'All I'm interested in is having someone help me who can handle the job without chasing after me every two minutes for fresh orders. I'm trying to get down to some serious art-work again, but the riding school! Well, you run one! You must know how it is!'

'I certainly do!' Elaine smiled. An exhilaration was taking hold of her. She felt completely free of the past now, despite the fact that a host of new responsibilities were looming up before her. But it wasn't responsibility she was tired of, she realised. What she needed was a complete change of scene, which was what she had. It looked like becoming a very interesting summer!

'My place is not far from here,' he said, then, after a pause, added, 'Have you been in Cornwall before?'

'Never! But it's a place I've always wanted to visit. So when my mother died I took the opportunity to get away.'

'Your mother died recently?'

'Her funeral was yesterday!' Elaine fell silent for a moment, then went on to tell him something of her life, without mentioning that Carrie Williams was her mother.

'I can understand your desire to get away from it all for a time,' he commented when she again lapsed into silence. 'With Lee around, I never had the opportunity to run and hide after my wife died. Perhaps that is what I really needed! But I had to think of him.' He sighed and broke off, then went on, 'I do what I can for him, but it's hopeless for a man to try and be a mother as well as a father. My wife's sister, Margaret, lives in and takes care of the house and Lee, but she leaves much to be desired, I'm afraid.'

They were silent then, and Elaine took the opportunity to admire the scenery that was flashing by, still marvelling that she was indeed in Cornwall.

Presently the car slowed and she looked ahead. There was a turn-off on the left, and he smiled at her as he swung the car down the green lane.

'Not far now. Our place is just short

of the cliffs, but a lot of the surrounding ground belongs to us, plus farm buildings and meadows. We have a dozen horses. How many do you have?'

'Fifteen, not including my own,' she responded.

'Will you consider bringing your own horse down here for the summer?'

'That's a thought. I'll miss Cleo badly.'

'Cleo?' He glanced at her, interest in his dark eyes.

'Cleopatra! She's something of a character. It might do her good to miss me for a while.'

'I think I know what you mean.' He smiled. 'I love horses! It's just that everything seems to have got on top of me at the moment. I haven't been able to settle down to what I really want to do, so I've been getting a bit up-tight.'

Ahead on the left there was a cluster of buildings, and, as they drew nearer, individual buildings began to take shape. There was a beautiful red-brick farm house that faced the distant cliffs, and extensive gardens that had the colours and delicate shades of spring flowers showing vividly.

Adrian brought the car to a halt in front of the house and gravel crunched under the tyres. Evening was pulling in, Elaine noted. Shadows were beginning to fill the corners. But she gained a sensation of rugged attractiveness and appreciated it as she alighted and turned to survey her surroundings.

A boy aged about eight suddenly emerged from the house and came bounding forward like a playful puppy. He was tall for his age, and lean, with dark hair and a face which resembled the man now standing at Elaine's side.

'Miss Carson, this is my son Lee. He was most insistent that I come and see you after hearing Michaela talking about you. If it hadn't been for Lee I doubt I would have plucked up the courage to come to the hotel.'

'Hello, Lee,' Elaine greeted as the boy grinned. 'So you like horses too, eh?'

'Very much, miss!' he replied, glancing at his father, and then he asked rather anxiously. 'Are you going to work here with us?'

'It's a distinct possibility,' she answered. 'From what I've heard about it, and seen already, I'd say this is the most beautiful place in Cornwall.'

'We'll show Miss Carson around, shall we?' Adrian suggested. 'You lead the way, Lee.'

The boy turned obediently and ran ahead. Elaine gazed after him, touched by a pang of sympathy because his mother was dead. They walked to the left, following a path that skirted the house. A side door opened suddenly and a woman appeared in the doorway. She halted and stared expressionlessly at Elaine, a short woman, probably in her 30s, with a sharp face and glinting brown eyes.

'My sister-in-law, Margaret,' Adrian said when they were abreast of the woman.

'How do you do?' Elaine responded.

'Hello!' There was grudging civility in the woman's tone. She was wearing jeans and a white blouse.

'This is Miss Carson,' Adrian went on, smiling at Elaine. 'If she decides to come and work with us then all our troubles will be over!'

The woman nodded and turned to enter the house again. Lee called from a gateway, and Elaine turned her attention to the boy. He was waving her on. She was inclined to take the job here without further discussion. There was something about Adrian Curtis that reminded her of herself, and she felt that if she could give a helping hand to anyone in need then she would also be helping herself.

'Well, what do you think?' Adrian asked hopefully, after they had completed a circuit of the school. 'Do you think you'd be happy working here?'

'I'm certain I would,' she replied without hesitation, and Lee, who was standing nearby, let out a whoop of delight. 'I'd love to come and do what I can.'

'Then let's get down to details.' Adrian smiled, and she warmed to him. He was evidently turning a brave face to the world, and she admired him for it. 'Lee, run into the house and ask Aunt Margaret to put the kettle on.' He glanced at Elaine as the boy departed obediently. 'You'll have a cup of tea or coffee before I take you back to town, won't you?'

'I'd love to!' She was relieved because she had committed herself, for now she had a good reason for staying in the area, and in three weeks she would come face to face with her mother!

4

The next morning at nine, Elaine entered the antique shop and presented herself to Frank Templeton, who greeted her cheerfully.

'Well, it didn't take you long to get caught up in local affairs, did it?' he remarked.

'I'm sorry if it upsets your plans at all,' she replied. 'But you did send Mr Curtis to see me at the hotel, didn't you?'

'Yes, and I said it would be all right if you worked mornings only for me. So how did you get on last evening? Are you going to work at the riding school? It was all I heard from Michaela when I got home.' He smiled encouragingly.

'Yes. When I finish here this morning I'm going out to the riding school,' Elaine confirmed. 'It looks like the start of a very busy summer!'

'When you're trying to recover from one of life's hard knocks it's good to be able to keep busy. I feel sorry for Adrian. He's been having a bad time of it. Did he tell you about his wife?'

'Yes. A tragic business! I just hope I'll be able to make matters easier for them!'

'I'm sure you will!' Frank nodded. 'And I have a message for you from Michaela. She has a free afternoon from school and she'd like you to take her to the riding school when you leave here.' He shrugged. 'She is rather imperious with her commands, and if you find that she gets a bit too much then just put her in her place.'

Elaine smiled. Michaela was her half sister! She considered that fact as she set to work under Frank's guidance, and a pang of anticipation stabbed through her. In three weeks, she thought, she would finally come face to face with her real mother!

Time seemed to fly then, for the work she undertook was absorbing. She loved the antiques, dusting and handling them with care and great pleasure. Frank made coffee about ten-thirty, and by noon, Elaine was getting the hang of things. But they had not seen a single customer, and Frank smiled when she remarked on that fact.

'Not to worry! These days, I don't expect anyone during the week. Mainly, this time of the year, I go around and buy in readiness for the summer season, but the shop has to remain open in case someone drops by. This is a strange business, and it takes some getting used to. But I think you'll be all right, Elaine. You're a natural for this kind of work.'

'I must admit that I like it, although I'm getting quite excited about going to the riding school this afternoon! Circumstances prevented me from running my own place for almost two years. And I didn't get many opportunities to ride for pleasure. But this summer I mean to change all that!'

'That's the way to talk! You must

always try to do your own thing.'

The shop door opened and the bell shrilled. Expecting her first customer, Elaine glanced over her shoulder and saw Michaela entering.

'Are you ready?' the girl called.

'I can't leave yet,' Elaine protested. 'I don't finish until one o'clock.'

'This is not good enough, Daddy,' Michaela said sternly, advancing upon her father. 'Elaine has to go to the riding school. If she can't save it I'll have nowhere to go to ride my pony, and what would Mother do with Juno?'

'Who told you that Elaine has to save the riding school?' Frank queried, smiling at Elaine.

'I talked to Lee at school this morning. He's excited! He said Aunt Margaret doesn't want Elaine to work there, and anything she doesn't want, Lee does.'

'There's some trouble between Lee and his aunt,' Frank explained to Elaine. 'I think she's trying to step into his mother's shoes! But the boy doesn't like her.'

'She doesn't like Lee!' Michaela said sharply. 'She picks on him all the time! He told me he'd run away if he could take his pony.'

'Well, Adrian certainly has his share of problems, don't you agree, Elaine?' Frank waved a hand. 'You'd better leave now! It wouldn't do to keep Michaela standing around in the shop. She'd almost certainly break something! I'd rather turn a wild bull loose in here!'

'Thank you.' Elaine smiled as she picked up her handbag. 'If you're ready, Michaela, we'll be on our way.' She paused. 'How do you get home from the riding school later?' she asked.

'You'll drive me,' came the quick reply, and Frank chuckled as Elaine escorted the girl outside.

When they were driving from town, Michaela began to ask questions about Elaine's home, and Elaine answered them as fully as she could.

'I don't know why you'd want to

come and live here with all that's going on for you back there,' the girl finally remarked.

'Perhaps it's difficult for a girl of ten to understand,' Elaine responded. 'Why don't you tell me something about your mother? Aren't you proud that she's a famous writer?'

'No! I wish she was just like any other mother! Then she wouldn't keep going away on business. But I'm luckier than Lee. His mother's dead!'

'Yes, so I heard: It must be heartbreaking for him. My mother is dead, and although I'm grown up, I miss her.'

When they reached the riding school, Lee was standing in front of the house waiting for them, and came running forward as the car drew up. He talked excitedly to Elaine, but as she alighted from the car and turned to get her riding clothes out of the back, Margaret appeared on the front step.

'Lee, I want you,' she called. 'I've asked you a dozen times to come and tidy your room. You'd better do it now or you'll get no tea.'

'Can't it wait a minute?' the boy demanded. 'I want to go with Michaela and Miss Carson. I want to see what they're going to do.'

'I'm going to ride my pony,' Michaela said. 'You'd better go and tidy your room or she won't let you out.'

'I tidied my room yesterday,' Lee protested. 'She's always telling me to tidy up.'

'Why don't you go now and get it over with?' Elaine suggested. 'I'm going to talk to your father before I do anything, and then I have to change into my working clothes. It will be half an hour at least before we start. Your room can't be all that untidy, can it?'

'All right.' He turned away reluctantly. 'But promise you won't do anything until I come.'

'I promise,' Elaine replied, and smiled when he darted away.

'You know what the trouble is with Margaret, don't you?' Michaela demanded as she and Elaine walked along the path to the stable.

'No.' Elaine shook her head.

'She wants to marry Adrian! That's why she stays here and looks after them. She doesn't like it here! She'd rather live in London! That's what she keeps telling Lee!'

'I see.' Elaine raised an eyebrow, and was relieved when Adrian emerged from the stable.

'Here you are then,' he commented, smiling. 'All ready to go to work?'

'All I need is a quiet place to change,' Elaine replied. 'I didn't get the opportunity in the shop. Someone turned up and dragged me away before it was time to finish.'

'And I can guess who that someone was,' he retorted. Then he frowned. 'Where's Lee? He's been haunting the front of the house for the past hour, waiting for you to show up.'

'Margaret called him. He's had to go and tidy his room,' Michaela said.

'Ah!' Adrian nodded. 'Well, he has to

learn to be tidy!' He glanced at Elaine. 'We'd better go over to the office and you can change there. Then I'll put you in the picture and let you get on with it.'

'I'm going to ride my pony,' Michaela said. 'Can Elaine ride with me this afternoon?'

'Yes! The first thing she should do is familiarise herself with her surroundings, which means she'll have to ride the bounds. You could show her around, couldn't you, Michaela?'

'I'd love to!' The girl nodded. 'I'll wait here, shall I? And bring Lee with you! If you don't ask for him he may not be able to come.'

'Why not?' Adrian frowned. 'He hasn't been naughty again, has he?'

Michaela shrugged and turned away, and there was a frown on Elaine's face as she accompanied Adrian to the house.

'I'm having a bit of trouble with Lee,' Adrian admitted. 'He's still missing his mother! That's why I don't like to be too hard on him. But it would be a mistake to pander to him just because he's motherless. Margaret keeps him well in hand.' He shrugged and added, 'I don't know what I'd do without her!'

Elaine did not reply, and they entered the house to hear Margaret shouting at Lee. The woman was standing at the foot of the stairs, but came towards them when she became aware of their presence.

'Is Lee playing up again?' Adrian asked.

'I'm making him tidy his room!' There was a tense expression in Margaret's dark eyes when she met Elaine's gaze.

'Elaine will take him and Michaela riding this afternoon, so send him over to the stable when he's finished here.' Adrian glanced at Elaine. 'The office is this way. I'll show you in and you can change.'

Elaine did not miss the scowl which came to Margaret's face as they turned away, and she was thoughtful as she entered the office and changed into her riding clothes. Adrian waited outside until she opened the door and presented herself to him. He looked at her appraisingly and nodded.

'You look the part perfectly!' he commented, smiling good-naturedly. 'I'm going to be busy this afternoon or I'd show you around, but you couldn't have better company than Michaela and Lee. They'll take good care of you.'

He crossed to the desk and pointed to an appointments book. 'There's no-one due for lessons this afternoon, and I'll be in my studio if someone should come making inquiries. You'll soon get into the routine. If you come in here whenever you arrive and check for appointments, you'll know how to arrange your time. There are some schoolgirls who help out after lessons. But I don't like too many youngsters around the place. That sort of thing could get out of hand. I expect you know that things are rather quiet at this time of the year, but during the summer we're so busy we don't know which way to turn.'

'It's the same where I live,' Elaine told him.

'Now what about a suitable horse for you to ride? I've thought about it, and I think you should ride Carrie Williams' horse, Juno. It's a lovely mare, and it doesn't really get enough exercise when Carrie is away on business.'

'What's she like?' Elaine asked as they went back to the stable.

'Carrie?' he nodded. 'A very nice woman! But you'll be seeing her around here quite a lot when she gets home. She loves horses, and Michaela takes after her.'

'Dad, can I come now?' Lee called from behind, and they turned to look for him. He was waving from an upstairs window.

Adrian smiled and waved in return. 'Come along then, and hurry! Tell Aunt Margaret I said you could.'

The boy's head disappeared immediately, and Elaine experienced a spasm of emotion in her breast as she considered the youngster's life. She glanced at Adrian to discover his gaze upon her.

'Your coming here seems rather like an act of God,' he remarked. 'Now I shall be able to get on with my own work. You're not going to have to do any manual work around here, you know. Tom Askew and his son Dick take care of that. All you have to do is give lessons, supervise the pony trekking, and keep the paperwork up to date.'

'It sounds like a good job!' she remarked, and half turned as Lee came running up. The boy inserted himself between Elaine and his father, and took hold of Adrian's hand.

'Did you check with Aunt Margaret before you came out?' his father asked.

'No, Dad, I forgot,' came the ready reply.

Adrian ruffled the boy's hair. 'All right. I'll tell her when I go back to the house.'

'Thanks, Dad!' Lee looked up at

Elaine, and she saw fresh hope in his eyes.

'You'll like it here, Elaine,' he went on, using her name for the first time. 'Aunt Margaret said she didn't think you'd be right for this place, but I think you will.'

'Did Aunt Margaret say that?' Adrian demanded, frowning.

'She's right to be cautious about a new face,' Elaine said, and Lee shot her a thankful glance.

'I'm ready to go,' Michaela announced when they entered the stable. The girl's black pony was champing some sweet-smelling hay, already saddled and bridled. 'I've saddled your pony, Lee, but I don't know which horse Elaine is going to ride so I couldn't do anything for her.'

'You've been busy,' Adrian commented. 'I'm going to put Elaine in charge of Juno, Michaela. That mare needs a lot more exercise than she's been getting.'

'What a good idea!' Michaela nodded.

'I'll bet Elaine can ride anything.'

Adrian smiled as he led the way to a stall farther along the stable, and Elaine's eyes gleamed with admiration when she saw the beautiful chestnut mare in the box. The animal snickered and pushed her muzzle forward to be stroked, and Elaine fondled it.

'What a beauty you are!' she exclaimed, rubbing the animal's ears. 'Juno! A very apt name for a very nice mare!'

She saddled and bridled the animal while Adrian watched with interest, and then led the mare out into the yard, where Michaela and Lee were already mounted and waiting. She swung lithely into the saddle and curbed the horse as it cavorted a little, impatient to be moving.

'Enjoy yourselves!' Adrian called, stepping back. 'I wish I could go with you but there's something I have to do. Michaela, show Elaine the gallops and the paths, and don't go too near the cliffs! I'll see you when you get back.'

Michaela and Lee maintained a carefree chatter as they departed. Elaine rode behind the youngsters, keeping the mare in check. They followed a path that led around the back of the stable, and then there was open ground before them. Michaela soon pushed her pony into a canter and Lee quickly followed suit. Elaine had difficulty keeping the mare in check, and she let the animal pull up alongside the ponies.

'Juno needs a run,' she said. 'I'll go on ahead for a short distance. You'll just have to follow me for a bit.'

'Show us how you can ride,' Michaela shouted.

Elaine smiled and urged the mare forward. The next instant she was galloping along the path at a terrific pace, and the wind whistled in her ears. Her pulses throbbed with excitement! Happiness filled her breast! This was more like it, she told herself.

When she reached the top of a rise the mare was blowing hard, and Elaine reined in and looked around for

Michaela and Lee. The youngsters were coming along steadily, and Elaine drew a deep breath and restrained it until her lungs began to protest. Then she exhaled in a rush. Her spirits were high for the first time in many months. There seemed to be a kind of magic in the air. She glanced at the cliffs to her left, saw the dark sea beyond, and raised her eyes to the heavens. Her prayers were being answered at long last!

Michaela and Lee arrived and reined in. Michaela slid out of her saddle and held the reins. Her cheeks were red, eyes gleaming. She looked a picture of health and happiness. Lee, on the other hand, was a bit pale, and his eyes were listless. Elaine frowned as she studied him, and warmed to him when he sensed her gaze and looked up and gave a little smile.

'Are you feeling all right, Lee?' she inquired.

'Yes, thanks.' He nodded. 'I had a cold last week, but I'm all right now.'

'He's not happy with his aunt,' Michaela said in a matter-of-fact voice.

'I really can't comment upon his home life,' Elaine said quietly. She stepped down from the high saddle and the mare immediately lowered her head and began to crop the turf. 'You know, Lee, if you don't antagonise your aunt then she would be much easier to live with.'

'He does everything she asks him!' Michaela was Lee's champion, and did not care who knew.

'Perhaps he should do everything the first time she asks,' Elaine suggested, 'and some things before she asks.'

'You don't know Aunt Margaret,' Michaela said darkly. 'Just wait until you do. Then you'll see!'

'Shall we ride on?' Elaine suggested, fearing that the conversation would get out of control. She held Michaela's pony until the girl had regained her seat and then remounted the mare. 'Let's canter,' she said. 'And we'd better not get too close to the cliffs! We can follow this path to that beautiful house up there. Who lives there, by the way?'

'I do,' Michaela said proudly. 'That's our house!'

They rode on, and dismounted to rest the horses when they reached the high wall that surrounded the big house atop its prominent rise overlooking the sea. Elaine looked across the expanse of the bay, noted the high, rugged cliffs, and realised that she had never seen a more attractive view.

'I've got a tree house behind the house,' Michaela said. 'If you want to come and look at it I'll take you in, Elaine.'

'Not right now,' Elaine decided. 'We have the horses with us. How far do you think we've come? Perhaps we ought to be starting back now.'

'No,' Lee pleaded. 'I don't want to go home yet.'

'There'll be other times when we can ride,' Elaine reassured him. 'We have to think of the ponies. They've brought you a long way.'

'We ride over here at least once a week,' Michaela said.

'Aren't there any other places you ought to show me before we ride back?' Elaine tried psychology, and it worked.

'Yes! There's the old mine!' Lee's eyes gleamed. 'We must show you that!'

'We've been told never to go there,' Michaela said sharply.

'Then we won't go!' Elaine spoke firmly. 'It's not wise to disobey orders.'

They mounted and rode on, and Elaine listened to the chatter of the children. From time to time she glanced at Lee, and tried to make up her mind about him. Obviously, he was not being physically ill-treated by his aunt. But there were other kinds of ill-treatment, and she determined to keep an eye on the situation.

The sun was well over into the western part of the sky when they finally returned to the stable, and Adrian was in the yard talking to two men. He turned at the sound of hooves, his serious expression being replaced by a smile when he saw them. The older of the two men touched his cap and moved away, while the younger, aged about 30, paused to throw a lingering look at Elaine.

'Did you have a nice time?' Adrian asked, coming to Elaine's side as she dismounted.

'Marvellous,' she replied.

'And the children behaved themselves?' He looked at Lee.

'They were extremely well behaved.' Elaine threw a glance at Lee, who smiled conspiritorially. His face seemed to have more colour now.

'Very well. Put your ponies away and take care of them.' Adrian took hold of Juno's reins. 'How did she behave with you in the saddle?' he asked.

'Perfectly! She's a beautiful animal!' Elaine patted the mare's arched neck. 'I've had a terrific afternoon.'

'Do you think you'll like it here?' He glanced at her, smiling.

'I'm sure I shall. But enough of my

slacking. I'd better set to work in earnest.'

'You're doing that already.' He nodded. 'I've managed to set foot in my studio for the first time in months, thanks to you.'

'But I haven't done anything yet!' she protested.

'I'd have had to exercise Juno if you hadn't,' he pointed out. 'But you'll have plenty to do very shortly.' He fell silent and turned as a shadow fell across them, and Elaine looked round and saw Margaret standing just behind her.

'You're wanted on the telephone, Adrian,' the woman reported. 'It's Edward Metcalfe, and he said he couldn't ring back later.'

'Thanks.' Adrian moved away instantly. 'Please excuse me, Elaine. I really must talk to Edward. I've been waiting for him to call.'

'I'll put Juno away,' Elaine responded.

Margaret remained while Adrian

went striding away across the yard to the house. Elaine sensed that the woman wanted to say something, and paused, waiting.

'I wish you hadn't come here,' Margaret said sharply.

'Really? Why is that?' Elaine countered.

'Because now Adrian will start making plans to keep this place going, and the best thing he could do is move to London and take up his career again. His wife is dead and he shouldn't bury himself here and turn the place into a shrine just because Sylvia loved it. But that's exactly what he's trying to do, and you're going to make matters worse!'

'From the way he talked, I thought I was doing the right thing by coming here!' Elaine frowned. 'He sounded like a man who needed help, and I was at a loose end. I'm sorry you should think like that, but there's nothing I can really do about it, is there?'

'You could decide that this isn't

what you want after all.' Margaret's dark eyes glittered. 'Why don't you go back to your own business and stop meddling in other people's lives? If you really want to help then leave Adrian alone.'

Elaine suppressed a sigh, and tried to think of a suitable reply, but Margaret turned on her heel and went back to the house, shoulders stiff and chin jutting. Elaine stared after her, wondering exactly what was in Margaret's mind, and a frown clouded her expression as she considered. Then Michaela spoke at her back, and Elaine glanced over her shoulder to see the girl and Lee standing by the water trough. She knew by their faces that they had overheard Margaret's words.

'She doesn't seem to like you either, Elaine,' Michaela said, a scared expression on her flushed face. 'But don't be afraid of her! She's just like the wicked witch of the west, and everybody knows that she always gets beaten.'

Elaine smiled, but the sight of Lee's

worried face sobered her. She moistened her lips as she searched for the right words.

'This isn't a fairy tale, Michaela,' she said quietly. 'For all we know, Margaret may have a very good reason for wanting the family to move back to London, and perhaps my presence here is wrong for everyone.'

'No!' Lee cried, and his face was paler than it had been earlier. 'I don't want to leave here and neither does Daddy. You mustn't go, Elaine! There's no-one else who can help us!'

'All right, I'll reserve judgment until I know more,' Elaine mused. 'There is work for me to do, and I think I had better get on with it, don't you? What time do you have to go home, Michaela? I'll drive you when you have to leave.'

'It doesn't matter really. Daddy doesn't get home until six, usually, and Lorna will be in her room playing records. I'd rather be here with the horses, so stay as long as you like.'

Elaine smiled and turned her attention to work. She watered Juno and then led the animal into the stable, where she off-saddled and removed the bridle. Then she began to groom the horse, and her worried thoughts faded as she became immersed in her work. This was what she really loved doing, and nothing would ever usurp its place in her heart!

5

It was surprising, Elaine discovered, just how easily she slipped into the new routines both at the shop and the riding school. After that first day her interest was well and truly captivated, and the ensuing days passed quickly. She spent each morning in the shop, and promptly at one o'clock each day she jumped into her car and drove to the stable, where Adrian was waiting to hand over to her. She soon proved to him that she was expert in management and tuition, and by the end of the first week she had thoroughly settled into the job and felt as if she had been there always.

But it was with Adrian himself that her greatest progress was made. He quickly appreciated her worth, and was not loath to praise everything she did. When she had tidied up the office and put all the books and files in order he sang her praises to Margaret while the three of them sat drinking coffee one afternoon, and the woman muttered something that was practically unintelligible and stalked off with the excuse that she had work to do.

'Margaret is a strange woman,' Adrian mused as the door slammed behind his sister-in-law. 'And she needs some understanding! I'm not at all happy with the set-up I have here. Margaret came to take care of Lee in the first place, and it was supposed to be a temporary arrangement. But she's deeply entrenched now and I don't understand how she can bury herself in a remote place like this and be happy.'

'You seem to be very happy here,' Elaine observed.

'Yes, but it takes a special kind of character to live like this, and, believe me, Margaret isn't the type.'

'Perhaps she doesn't like it but feels that she has a duty to you and Lee.' Elaine wanted to know more about the background to the situation that existed. 'I'm sure it's a thankless task, running this big house and taking care of two males.'

'You're right of course, and I do tend to forget that sometimes. A wife expects to be where ever her husband is, and usually helps him in his business, if she can. But Margaret came here because we had a tragedy, and she's made a good job of running things. Unfortunately she knows nothing about the business side of a riding school, and that's where I was coming unstuck.'

'Will you have to consider selling up and moving out?' Elaine queried.

He sighed and shook his head. 'I really don't know! I'd hate to let the place go because it was my wife's dream.' He paused and studied Elaine for a moment. 'I can see that you are the same type of woman as Sylvia. She was mad about horses, and you have the same kind of light in your eyes when you're handling or talking about them.'

Elaine smiled. 'I was lucky to have parents who owned horses.'

'It's strange that you walked out of your home just like that!' He looked at her with closer interest. 'Isn't there anyone back there who will miss you?'

Elaine shook her head even as she thought of Shaun. She had telephoned Mrs Kemp the day after her arrival, partly explained the situation, and gave the housekeeper the address of the hotel where she was staying. But she had not made any contact with Shaun, mainly because she did not want him questioning her movements, and partly because she hoped the separation would terminate anything that had existed between them.

'No,' she said slowly. 'There's no-one back there, really.'

'You sound as if you're not completely sure. Don't you have any family? I know you said your mother died recently. Is your father still living?'

'No. And they were not my real parents. I was adopted as a baby.'

'Really! And there were no other children in your adoptive family?'

'No. I was their only family.'

'And you had to nurse your mother through her terminal illness!' Adrian nodded. 'That sort of thing takes a lot out of you, doesn't it? No wonder you dropped everything and ran! But what about your business? Is everything being taken care of?'

'Certainly.' She nodded confidently. 'I don't have a thing to worry about.'

'And neither do I now!' He leaned back in his seat. 'Since your arrival I've managed to get my mind refocused on art. It's the first time since my wife died. I really ought to get a manager in to run this place so that I can concentrate upon my interrupted career.' He paused, then asked, 'Would you consider handling the job permanently?'

'Ordinarily I would jump at the opportunity!' She nodded. 'But I've reached a crossroads myself and I need a breathing space in which to think about everything that's gone before. That's why I left home. But there's no hurry for any kind of a decision, is there? I shall definitely be here until the end of the summer, which gives us about six months. Apart from that, I've only been here a week, and you may come to the conclusion before long that I'm not suitable.'

'Never!' He chuckled. But then his face sobered. 'You know, I am a bit worried about you,' he remarked.

'Really? Why?'

'You're working in the antique shop every morning and coming straight here every afternoon. You didn't have a day off this past week, and you put in a lot of extra time Saturday and Sunday.'

'Well, we were rather busy on Sunday,' she commented.

'I know that, and it's all very well buckling down to the job. But you won't be able to maintain that pace right through the summer! You must know that, with your experience. What do you usually do for relaxation? How do you spend your leisure time? Do you have any hobbies or pastimes?'

She shook her head. 'Horses have always been my ruling passion,' she admitted. 'There's never been time for anything else.'

'That's what they all say! But that sort of thing is all right if the business is your own. Back home you would be expected to handle everything and not count the hours. But here it is different. You'll have to get into a routine and stick to it. What do you do when you leave here, anyway? I'll bet you go into town and just sit in that hotel room!'

'Since I arrived I've been too tired to think of doing anything else,' she responded.

'You shouldn't be staying at a hotel either,' he said firmly. 'It must cost a pretty penny.'

'I don't have to worry about money! Which brings me to a timely change of subject. We're going to have to spend a great deal of money to bring certain areas of the school into line with the standards that are laid down for such places. How do you feel about that?'

'I agree. But at the moment cash is not flowing too freely.'

'Ten thousand pounds would be sufficient, I'd say.' Elaine opened a notebook. 'I've been making a few observations and calculations.'

He reached out and grasped her wrist, and suddenly his face was serious. She fell silent, surprised by his movement, and then he smiled and released her hand.

'I've never met anyone quite like you,' he said softly. 'You're just what is needed around here — a cold blast of reality to blow away any cobwebs and ghosts.' He paused and his lips twisted.

Then he nodded. 'Yes, ghosts! Or one ghost in particular! But three years have passed, and perhaps it takes that long to get over a tragedy.' He shook his head. 'All I do know is that since you've arrived I've had a great burden lifted from my mind and now I'm beginning to look to the future again.'

'Well, there you are!' Elaine smiled. 'So my coming to Cornwall was fateful after all!' Then she sobered. 'I must say that my coming here was the best thing I could have done. Already my own life is straightening out. It's a pity you couldn't have got away from here for a bit. A change of scenery works wonders.'

'There was more tying me to this place than you had at home, I expect,' he remarked. 'Lee, for one thing! But I've noticed how he seems to have perked up since your arrival, Elaine.'

'I've noticed that too! I must admit that I was worried about him at first.'

'But he's taken to following you everywhere, and I'm amazed at the changes around the house. These days, he clears up without being told, where before, Margaret was always snapping at him to put things away. And he's doing more around the stable! He's found himself a new interest, it seems.'

Elaine nodded. She had noticed how Lee had attached himself to her. He became almost a second shadow from the moment he came in from school.

'All he needed was a little understanding,' she said. 'Somehow, he seemed to find it in me. Give him a few weeks and you'll think he's a different boy altogether.'

'I hope he's getting over the death of his mother.' Adrian's tone hardened. 'It was bad enough for me! God knows what it was like for a little boy!'

Elaine silently agreed. She studied Adrian when he was staring across the room, and realised that in the week she had been here subtle changes had also taken place in her own mind. The passion to find her own mother, which had struck the instant she learned the truth of her adoption, had been pushed into the background by the situation evolving here at the riding school.

'You've turned very serious,' Adrian observed, and his voice dragged her back to reality. 'Not thinking about the past, are you? That's a bad thing! Look ahead all the time.'

'So what about the improvements that are needed?' She wanted to change the subject, and made a pretence of studying the figures she had jotted down in her notebook. A sudden thought struck her and she looked up at him, finding his gaze upon her. 'Have you considered taking a partner?' she demanded.

Surprise showed in his expression, and then he shook his head slowly. 'I don't think anyone would want to buy a share at this time. Mind you, I would jump at the chance of a working partner — someone who would manage the business side of it.'

'There is a type of person who wouldn't think twice about entering a partnership with you,' she said thoughtfully.

'Please go on!' He leaned forward attentively.

'Someone who is already in the business, who knows all about profit margins and that sort of thing.'

'Do you know anyone in that

category who might be interested in a quarter share of this business?' he inquired.

'A quarter share for something like ten thousand pounds?' she asked.

He gazed at her for some moments, and Elaine sat motionless, her pulses racing. Her intuition suggested that this moment would prove to be most significant. He nodded slowly.

'You're quite a businesswoman, Elaine. But you'd better think very carefully before plunging into something like this. You do have a business in Essex, and that has to be handled.'

'If you're prepared to give me a share for ten thousand then I'll certainly think about it, and take some legal advice,' she responded. 'What do you say?'

'Yes, with no hesitation.' He got up, a smile on his lips, and held out a hand to her. 'You now have an option to purchase a quarter share. Congratulations! Shall we drink to it?'

Elaine arose and took hold of his

hand. For a moment they looked into each other's eyes, and she felt a stab of emotion in her breast. Then he moved away, and she watched him cross to a drinks cabinet and pour amber liquid into two glasses. As he returned to her side she felt a trickle of tenderness in her heart, and suddenly she saw him in a different light, and her hand trembled as she touched his fingers in taking the glass from him. A lump came to her throat, and heat surged into her cheeks.

'Here's to a flourishing partnership,' he toasted, gazing steadily at her.

She smiled and chinked the rim of her glass against his. There was silence as they drank. Then Adrian took her glass and set it down.

'Please do take some advice on the partnership before you commit yourself,' he urged.

'I will, but it can only be a good investment, especially if I stay here and run things as we are doing now.' Her mind was leaping ahead, viewing possible snags and supplying instant solutions. 'I have a good manager back home, running the riding school there. I could slip back home this week-end to get things moving! Judith wants to get married, and Nick, her fiancé, is considering taking over my farm. He won't get married until he has settled in somewhere. I'll ring Judith this evening and set the ball rolling.'

'That's what I like about you!' He smiled. 'You don't let the grass grow under your feet.' He glanced at the appointments book. 'H'm, there's no-one due for a lesson until five. Shall we take a ride together? Juno needs some exercise, and I haven't been in the saddle since you arrived. I think it's about time we remedied that defect.'

Elaine nodded. 'I'd like that,' she said lightly. 'But I want to be back here when Lee and Michaela get home from school.'

'Margaret will bring Lee home from school just after four,' he calculated, glancing at his watch. 'That gives us ample time to ride.'

Elaine tried to analyse her emotions as they saddled up and then set out towards the cliffs. She rode Juno as usual, and Adrian was astride a powerful stallion. The sun was bright as they cantered, although the breeze was keen. When the path opened out, Adrian urged his horse into a gallop, and Elaine stretched out the mare to stay abreast of him. Her perception seemed to heighten as they raced along the springy turf. In the distance the sea glinted. The sky was blue, cloudless, and there were the odours of the sea and the countryside mingled to inflame her senses.

When the mare began to tire, Elaine reined in immediately. Adrian went on for another 50 yards before the stallion decided to slacken pace, and then he sat the animal and waited for Elaine to reach him.

'That was exhilarating,' she declared.

'Someone ought to take you around on foot and show you the sights,' he observed. 'In fact, I think I ought to start doing something about your leisure time. I believe in the saying that you should never flog a willing horse. Perhaps we can go out together in the evenings, Elaine. I don't know what you like doing for relaxation, but they cater for most tastes around here.'

'Thanks. I would appreciate some company in the evenings. It is rather boring sitting alone in a hotel room.'

'Then let's make an early start!' He smiled as she regarded him. 'I'll call for you at seven-thirty this evening.'

'Fine! But I shall need to make some telephone calls when I get finished for the day. I will go home this week-end, if that's all right with you. I must get something sorted out at that end.'

'Certainly! Take as long as you like! I'll be on the place all week-end.' He glanced at his watch. 'We've got time to go on a bit farther, if you like. I'd love to show you some of the sights that people come from all over the world to see.'

'If we have the time then you'll get

no complaints from me,' Elaine responded. She breathed deeply as they went on, aware of her fluttering pulses and the heady sensation that began enveloping her. Adrian seemed to be getting more attractive by the minute, and suddenly realisation came, as quickly as if scales had fallen from her eyes and mind.

Two riders appeared on the path ahead just before they sighted the riding school, and Adrian chuckled when he pointed to them.

'Look who's coming,' he said.

Elaine saw Michaela and Lee jogging along, and a sigh escaped her. She had come to Cornwall and intruded into another world! It was impossible to walk into the lives of people without becoming involved with them to some degree, she realised, and here she had plonked herself in the middle of a situation that could get out of hand. If she had to leave suddenly then Lee at least would get hurt! She looked at Michaela, and felt a rush of emotion.

Her half-sister! Then she thought of Carrie Williams, and wished that her mother would hurry back from her business trip.

Should she confide her secret to Adrian? She glanced at him as they reined in to greet the children. But it wouldn't be fair to Carrie to tell anyone before her mother was aware of the fact herself! She fought against the impulse and smiled at the children.

'We thought you'd gone away and left us!' Lee shouted as soon as he was within earshot.

'I didn't think that at all,' Michaela retorted. 'I know Elaine isn't going to leave.'

'Not for a long time,' Elaine said, smiling. 'But I have to go home this week-end. Some business has come up which I can't handle from here.'

'Going home?' Lee's expression changed instantly. 'You'll come back again, won't you?'

'Of course I will! I'll be gone about two days. If I leave on Friday evening I should be back on Sunday. You won't even have time to miss me!'

'There are some people you can miss if you don't see them for five minutes,' Adrian said jocularly. 'Isn't that right, children?'

Both Michaela and Lee agreed vociferously, and Elaine smiled. But some of her pleasure fled when Lee spoke about Margaret.

'I had trouble getting out,' he said. 'Aunt Margaret said I had to go to town with her, but I didn't want to go, so she went off in a mood.'

'You always go into town with her on a Tuesday,' Adrian said. 'That's when she does the weekly shopping, and you like to help her.'

'I don't really help,' Lee said firmly. 'Half the time she says I'm a nuisance and I get in her way! So I thought I'd let her go alone this time. Then she can't blame me for anything.'

As they talked, the children turned their ponies and began to ride back the way they had come. Elaine remained in the background, aware that Lee constantly looked at her. But she recognised that there was a void in his life, and if he needed her to fill it then she could only accept the honour gracefully.

When they had unsaddled, Adrian went into the house and Elaine began to handle some of the chores that had to be done before she could finish for the day. There was one riding lesson to be given, and Lee went with her when she accompanied the teenaged pupil. He remained in the background, silent and unobtrusive until the lesson was over.

'I'd like to learn to jump my pony over hurdles,' he remarked after the pupil had gone. 'Would you teach me, Elaine?'

'Certainly. But can your pony jump hurdles? If she cannot then she'll have to be schooled.'

'She can. Michaela sometimes jumps for me. I've tried it but I always fall off.'

'You ride very well so I'm sure you'll be able to jump with no trouble at all,'

Elaine told him. 'We'll have to wait until after the week-end, Lee. Then I'll start teaching you.'

'I wish you didn't have to go home,' he said mournfully.

Elaine frowned as she glanced at him. 'Cheer up,' she said, digging him playfully in the ribs. 'I'll be back again in two days. In fact that will hardly be enough time for what I need to do. Just look forward to Monday, when your lessons begin.'

He cheered up slightly at that and they went into the barn, where Tom Askew was working. Lee went over to talk to the man, and Elaine continued her chores.

Just before she was due to leave for the day, Lee came back to her, and held her hand as they walked towards the house. Michaela appeared from the rear paddock. A car was coming along the drive, and Michaela let out a cry when she saw it.

'Lorna's here,' she cried, 'and I'm not ready to go home yet.'

Elaine looked curiously at the girl who got out of the car. She was slim and pretty. This was Michaela's sister, her half-sister! Lorna was about 21, and attractive. Michaela ran to the girl, grasped her hand, and they turned and walked towards Elaine.

'This is my sister, Lorna,' Michaela introduced. 'She's too big to ride a pony now. She thinks it's a kid's pastime. Lorna, this is Elaine. I've told you all about her.'

'Hello, Elaine!' Lorna smiled. 'I hope my brat of a sister doesn't make too much of a nuisance of herself around here.'

'Hello, Lorna.' Elaine shook her head. 'No, Michaela is quite useful around here.' She saw Michaela smile approval but she could not take her eyes off Lorna, for the girl had a great resemblance to herself, except that their general colouring was different. But Elaine could see certain similarities, and half wondered why Michaela did not spot them.

'Are you ready to go home yet?' Lorna demanded. 'You're always such a pest to pick up because you never know when to leave here. I have to go out this evening, and Daddy wants you in the house when he gets home, for a change. So say goodbye to your friends and we'll start back.'

'You always spoil all the fun!' Michaela complained, and came to Elaine's side. 'Tomorrow, will you wait for me before you take Juno out on exercise?'

'Yes.' Elaine patted the girl's shoulder.

She and Lee stood and waved as Michaela was driven away, and then Elaine took hold of Lee's hand and led him into the house. Margaret came to the kitchen door and stared at them, then turned on her heel and went back to her chores. The sound of a typewriter clattering indicated the whereabouts of Adrian, and Elaine walked to the door of the office and peered in. Lee remained with her, gripping her hand tightly.

'It's time I departed, if I'm to be ready to go out at seven-thirty,' she said.

Adrian looked up from the desk and smiled. He glanced at Lee, noted the way the boy stayed with Elaine, and got to his feet.

'We'll see Elaine off the premises, shall we, Lee? Then we'd better get cleaned up and have some tea.' He smiled at Elaine as they left the office, and she caught her breath, for he seemed to get more handsome each time she saw him.

6

By the time Friday afternoon had arrived, Elaine was mentally confused, and quite emotional. Now she could not look at Adrian without wanting to be close to him and her feelings intensified with each passing day.

Adrian had taken her out on the Tuesday evening, and she had been enchanted by his personality and appeal. They had dined in the best hotel in town, and afterwards danced in a night club. The evening had passed like a dream, and afterwards they had agreed to go out again. Now Elaine could hardly wait for Sunday to come so that she could get back and see him again.

But this afternoon seemed to drag! Adrian had gone into town, and Elaine had two lessons to take. By three-thirty both pupils had gone, and she went across to the house to attend to the office work. She had decided that as soon as Michaela and Lee arrived she would leave and start the long journey to Essex. But she had hardly sat down at the desk when the door opened and Margaret peered in.

'I think it's about time we had a talk,' Margaret said harshly, entering and closing the door. She moved to the seat beside the desk and dropped into it, eyes upon Elaine, her face showing determination and a host of mingled emotions.

'What's wrong?' Elaine countered, leaning back in her seat and suppressing a sigh.

'I don't know what's in your mind, but if you are after Adrian then you'd better think again! I haven't been here for three years, slaving away seven days a week, just to lose him now. You've only just come on the scene and already you've got everyone eating out of your hand, except me.

'I can't do a thing with Lee, and

110

Adrian is acting like a schoolboy! I wanted him to leave here and go to London, and he was beginning to think along those lines when you came and put other ideas into his head. This is no life for him! He can never be really happy here! And I don't want to be stuck here for the rest of my life!'

'I don't know what you're getting at,' Elaine said quietly. 'I came because I was asked to help out, and that's all I've done. I'm sorry if that doesn't meet with your approval, but Adrian will do what's best for him and for Lee. I wouldn't try to dissuade him now and neither should you.'

'They're talking about you becoming a partner! If you have that kind of money to throw away then you're lucky. But I think it's not the riding school you're interested in! You're after Adrian!'

'That's not true!' Elaine shook her head, although she was painfully conscious of the fact that her heart was thudding madly.

'But if he became attracted you wouldn't turn away from him, would you?' Margaret leaned forward, glaring. 'So I'm warning you off! Stay away from Adrian! He's mine! I've put in a lot of time and work to get him, and I won't lose him now.'

Margaret got to her feet and moved to the door, where she paused and glanced over her shoulder, face screwed up with anger and eyes glinting. 'Why don't you go back to where you came from and stay there?'

Elaine gasped as Margaret departed, for Lee was standing in the background, staring at her in horror, having heard Margaret's outburst. But she was so immersed in her own conflicting feelings that the sight of him did not register for the moment, and then he turned and darted away before she could stop him.

Heaving a sigh, Elaine returned to her work, and forced herself to bring the ledgers up to date. But Margaret's words were gyrating madly in her mind, and she was thankful that she was getting away for the week-end. She eventually finished and left the house to go in search of the children, finding Michaela in the stable, grooming her pony. There was no sign of Lee.

'Michaela, have you seen Lee?' Elaine called, and the girl looked up.

'I saw him across the yard ten minutes ago. He seemed upset about something and didn't answer when I called him. I think he went into the barn. That's his favourite place when he's upset and missing his mother and wants to be alone.'

'I'm leaving soon to go home for the week-end,' Elaine said, 'and I want to say goodbye to Lee.'

'I'll miss you,' Michaela said quietly. 'Things have been different around here since you came.'

Elaine smiled. 'I'll miss you, too!'

'I wish Lorna was more like you.' Michaela was suddenly very serious. 'She never takes the trouble to be nice to me. I'm only her younger sister!'

'The age gap makes it difficult,' Elaine said gently, smiling.

'But you're not like that! You listen to me! And you're trying to help Lee. I can't imagine Lorna wanting to help anyone.'

'Never mind!' Elaine turned away. 'Tell Lee I'll see him when I get back on Sunday. I have to be going now.'

'I'll walk you to your car.' Michaela came and got hold of Elaine's hand. 'Did you say goodbye to Adrian?'

'I saw him earlier. He went into town and won't be back until later.' Elaine glanced around as they crossed the yard, but there was no sign of Lee. 'I really ought to see Lee before I leave,' she said. 'I think he was upset by something he overheard Margaret say.'

'She's always upsetting him!' Michaela drew Elaine on towards the car. 'Don't worry about him. I'll talk to him when you've gone.'

Elaine nodded as they reached her car. She had packed a week-end bag and put it in the boot, and had arranged with Frank to have Saturday morning off. Acting upon an impulse, she bent and kissed Michaela on the cheek, and the girl smiled and clung to her for a moment.

'It won't be the same around here until you get back,' she said as Elaine opened the car door.

Elaine glanced back as she edged the car into the drive, and saw Michaela waving madly. She accelerated, and a sigh escaped her when the house finally disappeared from her rear view mirror. She settled down to driving and mentally composed herself for the long journey.

She drove steadily, and when darkness fell she began to look for a petrol station. Turning on the car radio, she kept herself alert by listening to a news programme. When she saw the lights of a garage she turned off the road and drew in at the pumps. But as she opened her door to alight there was a sound from the back seat. She twisted to see Lee rising up and rubbing his eyes!

'Lee!' For a moment she was flabbergasted, and he stared at her silently. 'What on earth are you doing in the back?'

'I've been asleep,' he said, still rubbing his eyes.

'That I can see!' She opened the rear door and slid into the back seat beside him. 'I don't believe this,' she commented. 'You knew I was going home for the week-end, didn't you? And what about your father? They must have missed you at home!'

'I thought you wouldn't come back on Sunday,' he said. 'And I couldn't stay with Aunt Margaret any longer. I heard what she said to you!'

Elaine pulled him into her arms and hugged him. He began to cry and she patted his shoulder as his body shook with emotion.

'Don't worry, everything will be all right.'

She talked gently and consoled him until Lee quietened; and summoning up his dignity drew away from her.

'Are you hungry?' she asked. 'But you must be! You didn't have any tea, and I've been on the road for hours. Hey, I'd better call your dad and let him know you're with me.'

'Are you going to take me back home now,' he asked as they got out of the car.

'Let me get some petrol! You go into the shop and buy some chocolate, if you're hungry. I'll be in shortly.'

She watched him as she put petrol in the tank, and a tender smile touched her lips. What was she going to do with him? He looked so forlorn! She locked her filler cap and entered the shop.

'Would you like to go home with me for the week-end?' she asked.

'Yes, please!' His forlorn expression vanished immediately and he grinned and came to take her hand. 'I'd love that! Then I wouldn't miss you. Michaela said you wouldn't take me back if you didn't find me too close to home.'

'Oh, did she?' Elaine bent and kissed his cheek, and smiled as she straightened. 'Let me pay for the petrol and then I'll call your dad. He must be frantic, unless Michaela told him where you are!'

'She said she wouldn't because she might get into trouble.'

'Well, I don't think there will be any trouble! But your poor father must be extremely worried right now.' Elaine paid for her petrol and then selected some chocolate bars and biscuits for Lee.

'That's the best I can do until we reach home,' she said. 'Now where's the payphone? Ah! Come with me.'

She dialled the number of the riding school, a faint smile on her lips as she noted Lee's sheepish expression. But she was actually pleased that he was with her! And the knowledge came as something of a shock! In fact, if she had given any thought to it earlier, she would have asked him along as a matter of course.

'Hello?' Adrian's voice sounded in her ear, and she grinned at Lee to reassure him.

'Adrian, it's Elaine,' she replied.

'Elaine! This is a surprise! But I'm glad you've called! I have a crisis on my hands. Lee has gone missing! We searched everywhere before dark and there's no sign of him!'

'He's with me! I've only just found him! He was asleep in the back of my car, lying on a horse blanket.'

'Thank God!' Adrian's voice was muffled at the other end of the line. 'You didn't know he was in the back?'

'No. He snuggled down under the blanket and fell asleep when I moved off.'

'Just wait until I see him!' Adrian promised. 'Are you bringing him back? Where are you exactly?'

'Too far along the road to want to turn back now! If it's all right by you I'll take him with me.'

'Certainly, it's all right by me! But you have business to discuss this week-end, and you won't want him hanging around.'

Elaine was watching Lee's face, and saw a host of expressions flit across it while she had been talking to Adrian. Now he was gazing at her, hopeful yet sad, and she smiled. She knew she did not have the heart to disappoint him.

'He'll stay with me,' she said firmly. 'He won't be any trouble. It seems as if he's decided that he should spend the week-end with me, so who am I to say no?'

'That's awfully good of you, Elaine! You could drop him off at the nearest police station and I'd pick him up.'

'I wouldn't dream of it! Besides, I'd like him to see my home and the riding school. He's been asking questions about the place ever since I came to work for you.'

'Well, tell him that he'll get it in the neck when I do catch up with him,' Adrian retorted with mock severity.

'I shall do nothing of the kind! He's going to be my guest for the week-end.

You can expect to see him on Sunday, probably in the evening.'

'All right, and thank you, Elaine. We'd better hang up now. I must ring the local police and tell them that he's safe. Have a nice week-end.'

'I'm sure we'll do that! Goodbye!' She chuckled and hung up.

'Was he very angry?' Lee asked cautiously.

'No. Just relieved that you're safe and well. But we won't talk about that now. We'd better get on. There's still a long way to go, and I'm sure you're hungry.'

'I'm not really,' he said. 'I'm too excited.'

Elaine chuckled as they went back to the car. She settled him in the back seat with the biscuits and some chocolate. Then they continued, and there was silence while Lee ate some of the biscuits.

'I won't be a nuisance,' he said suddenly. 'And thank you for letting me go with you.'

'I didn't have much choice, did I?' she countered.

'Well, you could have taken me back but you didn't,' he said, and fell silent again.

It was almost eleven o'clock when she turned off the A12 and drove along a minor road to her home. Darkness pressed in around them, and she felt very tired. Then she saw the farmhouse, the lights in the front windows welcoming her, and heaved a shuddering sigh as she brought the car to a halt at the front door.

'Are we there?' Lee was instantly awake and peering over the seat at her side.

'Yes, this is the place I call home,' she replied, and for a moment there was a secret wish in-her heart. She wished that Adrian was here with her! She stifled a sigh and opened the car doors. 'Come on, I think we should try to find you a bed for the night, shouldn't we? Although you've slept most of the way.'

'I'm not tired,' he said seriously. 'I

sometimes stay up late and watch TV.'

The front door opened and Mrs Kemp appeared in the doorway. 'Did you have a good trip?' she demanded, and then caught sight of Lee. 'Hello, who is this?'

'I'm Lee Curtis! Elaine works for us.'

'I didn't know he was coming with me until the last moment, Mrs Kemp,' Elaine said, 'or I would have telephoned and asked you to prepare a bed for him.'

'It's no bother.' Mrs Kemp chuckled. 'Come inside! We can soon fix him up.'

'In the room next to mine please,' Elaine said as she dragged her case out of the car boot.

Mrs Kemp took charge of Lee, and he disappeared into the upper regions of the house. Elaine sat down in the lounge and tried to relax. She glanced at the telephone, and could not resist the impulse to call Adrian. She dialled his number, and her heartbeats quickened as she awaited a reply. Then Adrian spoke.

'It's only me,' she announced. 'I thought you'd like to know that we have arrived safely, and Lee has just gone up to bed.'

'I'm glad you did think to ring me! I've been wondering how you were getting along. It's a long drive, isn't it?'

'Yes. But it wasn't too bad. I had some company on the last lap.' She chuckled.

'I hope he'll behave himself. But what a thing to do! I was worried sick when he didn't show up at dusk. Why did he do it, did he say?'

'Not really! Perhaps he just wanted a change of scenery! I wouldn't be too hard on him when he comes back, Adrian.'

'Well, I mean to have a talk with him because the local police sergeant saw Michaela when we had no idea where Lee was, and she said she thought he had run away from home because Margaret ill-treats him!'

'Really!' Elaine set her teeth into her bottom lip for a moment. 'He hasn't said anything of that nature to me. Have you questioned Margaret?'

'No! What could I say to her? I'll wait until Lee comes home and then have a chat with him. I do know that Margaret has been getting moody lately. Perhaps her life here has become a bit too much. But I'll let it simmer over the week-end.'

'Yes, I would if I were you! We'll see you on Sunday then. I'm tired now. I'm going to take a shower and then tumble into bed.'

'Sleep well,' he responded. 'And thanks again, Elaine.'

'Think nothing of it,' she responded lightly, but her heart ached strangely as she pictured his face. Now she was wishing that she hadn't suggested coming home this week-end! She paused for a moment and then continued. 'You know, I think Lee came with me because he was afraid I wouldn't come back to Cornwall. And I'm sure he's feeling insecure because of his mother's death. He's obviously been missing her terribly, but probably hasn't had the opportunity to express his feelings until now. It sometimes happens like that, and if that is the reason then this will have done him a lot of good.'

'I'm sure you're right. We'll have a chat when I see you again. Good-night, Elaine. And tell Lee in the morning that he needn't worry about coming home.'

'I'd tell him that in any case,' she said, chuckling. 'Good-night, Adrian.'

She hung up and sat for a moment reflecting upon the situation. Mrs Kemp came silently into the room.

'He's asleep already, poor lad!' the housekeeper remarked. 'He's a nice young lad, Elaine.'

Elaine explained something of the circumstances, and Mrs Kemp chuckled.

'He's probably adopted you as a mother-figure,' she said. 'You'll have to be careful how you handle him after this. It's too easy to break a child's heart.'

'You've told Judith and Nick that I'm coming home this week-end?' Elaine changed the subject.

'Indeed! They'll be here at ten in the morning to talk to you.'

'And you spoke to Mr Morley?'

'Oh, yes! He said he doesn't normally work on a Saturday but he'll make an exception for you. He'll be here around eleven in the morning, on his way to the golf course.'

'Good. I won't take up much of his time. I want to get things settled one way or another.' Elaine stifled a yawn. 'I think I'll take a shower and go to bed. All that driving has made me tired.'

'By all accounts you're leading a hectic life in Cornwall,' Mrs Kemp observed. 'Your eyes look heavy, Elaine. You're not doing too much, are you? Nursing your mother was a very strenuous business, and such an emotional strain. You must give yourself time in which to recover, you know.'

Elaine thought of the tears she had shed back in the car, aware that she was now feeling much better than before. She nodded as she went up to her room. One could never stand still in any situation, she thought wisely, and felt that she had made good progress since the funeral.

She showered and then tumbled into bed, and knew nothing more until the morning. When the sun peeped in at her window she opened her eyes and looked around at familiar surroundings. She had grown up in this room! A cockerel crowed outside, and she sat up and hugged her knees. This was home! But her heart was no longer in it! She had laid the foundations of another life in Cornwall, and now she felt alienated from this familiar scene. Home was where the heart is, she told herself, and knew that her heart was firmly entrenched in Cornwall!

Glancing at her watch, she noted that the time was almost nine, and threw back the bedcovers and hurriedly arose. Pulling on a dressing gown, she went to Lee's room and peeped inside, to discover that he was not there. She went back to her own room and hastily pulled on jeans, a sweater and a pair of trainers. Hurrying down to the kitchen, she paused upon opening the door, for Lee was eating breakfast at the table, and telling an attentive Mrs Kemp all about Cornwall.

'Shaun called a few minutes ago,' Mrs Kemp said as she arose to put the kettle on.

Elaine frowned. 'Did you tell him I was home?'

'Didn't you want me to?' Mrs Kemp threw a quizzical glance at her. 'I'm sorry, I didn't know you didn't want to see him! I told him you were here for the week-end, and he's coming over in an hour.'

'Judith and Nick will be here at ten!' Elaine turned to go back to her room, then paused. 'Lee, will you be able to amuse yourself for a little while? I have a great deal to do this morning, but after that I'll have plenty of time for you.'

'He'll be all right with me,' Mrs Kemp said, and Lee nodded.

By the time Elaine had breakfast it was almost 10, and she took Lee into the lounge to await her callers. She had hardly sat down when there was the sound of a car drawing up outside. She ran to the window, peered out, and caught her breath when she saw it was Shaun. She watched him alight and approach the house, and frowned. He seemed more like a stranger than ever! The doorbell rang, and a moment later Mrs Kemp opened the door to him. Elaine listened to his voice and felt a wave of reluctance overwhelm her. But the next moment the lounge door was opened and Shaun peered into the room.

'Hello!' He came forward quickly, but she did not rise to greet him. 'I've missed you! Are you home for good?' He paused, spotting Lee, who remained silent and watchful at Elaine's side. 'Who's this?' he demanded. 'Not someone you've adopted, is it?'

'I'm Lee,' the boy said instantly. 'Elaine works for my dad.'

'The antique shop!' Shaun nodded, then moved to Elaine's side and sat down on the settee.

'Not the antique shop! That's Michaela's.' Lee shook his head. 'We have the riding school!'

'Riding school?' Shaun frowned as he glanced at Elaine. He evidently saw some changes in her for he gazed more intently and seemed about to speak when she heard another car draw up outside. 'Ah! That sounds like Judith and Nick! They're right on time. I came home from Cornwall to see them, Shaun.'

'And not to see me, eh?' he demanded, his frown deepening.

'I don't have long! Mr Morley is coming to see me at eleven.'

'Well, I'll wait until you get through!' Shaun got to his feet, a bitter smile upon his face. He looked at Lee. 'Lee, isn't it?' He nodded. 'Why don't we go and look at the stables while Elaine is busy? Then you can compare it with the one you have in Cornwall.'

'I wish you'd leave and come back later,' Elaine said.

'Don't worry about us!' Shaun held out a hand to Lee, who glanced at Elaine for confirmation.

'Yes,' she said, 'you can go with Shaun. When I've talked business with these people I'll come out and show you around myself.'

Shaun held Lee's hand as they departed, and the next instant Judith and Nick entered the room.

'How did you find Cornwall?' Judith inquired. 'Mrs Kemp said you were enjoying yourself.'

'Cornwall is beautiful and perfect!' Elaine motioned to two seats. 'Come and sit down and we'll talk. I have to see Mr Morley at eleven, and we need to get certain matters sorted out before he arrives. I'm going back to Cornwall tomorrow,' She paused and smiled at Nick. 'Hello, Nick. Don't look so tense! This is just a friendly get-together.'

'Do I look tense?' He smiled. 'We're all very good friends, Elaine! But what is worrying is the fact that what we're about to discuss, and the decision we will make, is going to affect all of us for the rest of our lives.'

Elaine nodded and leaned back in her seat. She was aware of the implications, and her own life seemed to be lying very much in the balance. But she was quite prepared to burn her boats because it seemed to be the right thing to do . . .

7

It did not need many moments of discussion for Elaine to discover that Nick dearly wanted to take over the farm, and Judith was eager to continue managing the riding school. She was delighted, and shrugged off the business side of the takeover.

'I'm not going to worry about that aspect of it,' she said blithely. 'As you've said, we're very good friends, and Mr Morley will sort out the details. I leave it to you two to discuss the matter with him, and he will have my permission to accept any offer which is fair and reasonable. But I'd like to keep my interest in the riding school, Judith, if you are agreeable.'

'Certainly.' Judith nodded emphatically. 'I'll be happy to continue to run it under our current arrangement. It's more than fair to me.'

'Then let's have some coffee to celebrate the agreement, and if you'd care to wait for Mr Morley to arrive we could get some of the preliminaries attended to. As I'm going back to Cornwall tomorrow, and I expect to be staying there, I don't want to have to keep running backwards and forwards, so I need to settle my end of it. The general details can be ironed out as we proceed.'

'Are you going to live in Cornwall?' Judith asked.

'I don't know yet. There are certain events which cannot be settled at the moment. In time I'll be able to tell you all about it, I expect. But right now matters are rather up in the air.'

Mrs Kemp came in with a tray, and they drank coffee and relaxed. Shaun returned with Lee, who came to Elaine's side. She gave him some coffee, and Shaun sat down across the room, a tense smile upon his face. Studying him, Elaine saw that he was upset about something, and wondered what he had been asking Lee. The boy was quiet, and remained close to her.

'I've got a holiday due to me,' Shaun said suddenly. 'I was hoping we could go off somewhere, Elaine.'

'I couldn't possibly get away now!' She shook her head. 'I have certain commitments in Cornwall that will tie me there at least until the end of the summer.' She glanced at Lee, not wanting to say anything that might upset him or give him a wrong idea. 'And I really don't wish to discuss my future at this time, Shaun. Nothing is settled, so it's pointless trying to discuss it.'

'What is there to discuss anyway?' Shaun shrugged. 'You're your own mistress now. Have you met your mother yet?'

A silence followed his words, and Judith frowned as she glanced at Elaine.

'Did I hear right?' she asked. 'Shaun asked if you had met your mother!'

'Yes. That's right.' Elaine threw an angry glance at Shaun. 'It's not generally known that I was an adopted child. In fact, I didn't learn of it myself until after the funeral, and it was quite a shock. But since I've learned who my real mother is, I'm in Cornwall now to see her.'

'You haven't seen her yet?' Shaun demanded. 'Well, you've been away long enough! Don't tell me you're watching her from a distance!'

'Shaun, I've told you that I don't wish to discuss my affairs!' Elaine got to her feet.

'We'll leave if you like,' Judith said, rising also. 'We can come back at eleven to see Mr Morley.'

'There's no need for that!' Elaine shook her head. 'Shaun can leave! I don't have the time to see him this morning.'

Shaun got to his feet immediately, smiling wryly. 'I can take a hint,' he remarked. 'See you later then. Goodbye, Lee. I enjoyed our little talk. If I'm ever in Cornwall I'll come and see your riding school.'

Elaine frowned as Shaun departed, and when the door had closed behind him she glanced at Lee, who sat uncomfortably on the edge of his seat.

'Was Shaun asking you questions about Cornwall, Lee?' she asked.

'He wanted to know all about our riding school,' Lee responded, 'and what you were doing with us. You don't mind because I told him, do you, Elaine?'

'No, of course not! It doesn't matter at all.' Elaine smiled to allay his fears.

'I told him you were working in the antique shop every morning,' Lee went on. 'And that I hoped you'd marry my dad so you'd never leave us.'

Judith chuckled. Nick got to his feet and walked to the window. Elaine drew a deep breath and held it for a moment. Then she laughed.

'Well, I guess Shaun asked for that, didn't he?' She glanced at Judith, who smiled. Then she went to Lee's side and took his hand. 'You don't have to worry that I'll leave Cornwall,' she assured him. 'At the moment it looks as if I shall be living there for a very long time.'

Lee smiled and clutched her hand, and in that moment Elaine felt an instinctive deepening of her feelings for Lee and his father.

'Mr Morley is arriving,' Nick said, turning from the window.

The lawyer came bustling into the house. He was on his way to play golf and had no intention of staying long. Elaine had no wish to delay him longer than necessary and quickly explained the situation. Morley nodded.

'Yes,' he said. 'I can arrange that business with no trouble. I'll draw up some papers and then get you to sign them. It's as simple as that.' He glanced at Nick. 'Have you arranged to buy the farm? How are you raising the capital?'

'My father will foot the bill,' Nick replied. 'He told me to tell you to contact him when the preliminary details have been sorted out.'

'Fine.' Morley nodded. 'I'll put this

matter in hand first thing Monday morning.'

'I'm keeping my interest in the riding school,' Elaine said. 'The current arrangement with Judith will continue, Mr Morley. I shall remain in Cornwall for the time being, and you'd better have a couple of telephone numbers where you can reach me any day of the week. I'll write them down for you.'

'And your reason for being in Cornwall,' Morley said. 'Has that been settled to your satisfaction?'

'Not yet.' Elaine shrugged. 'She's out of the country at the moment. But there is another matter I wish to discuss with you when we've completed this business.'

Morley nodded, busily making notes. Then Judith and Nick took their leave, Elaine promising to call them in a few days. Lee looked forlorn, seated on the settee, and Elaine moved to his side and took hold of his hand.

'This is Lee Curtis, Mr Morley,' she said. 'His father owns a riding school in Cornwall, and I'm contemplating buying a quarter share for ten thousand pounds. Would you handle the details of that for me?'

Lee looked up at Elaine's words, and grinned. She met his gaze and nodded, happy because he seemed so relieved at her words.

'You're satisfied that a quarter share is worth ten thousand pounds?' Morley asked.

'Well, I'll leave it to you to arrange a valuation and then advise me,' she said. 'Would you do that?'

'Most certainly, and I wish you good luck in the venture. You do know all about that type of business.' Morley was keen to get away to his golf now.

Elaine nodded as she walked him to the front door. 'Thank you for everything, Mr Morley. I'm quite happy with the way everything is going now. Goodbye. Call me in Cornwall if any snags crop up. I'll want you to continue handling my affairs. Will you do that?'

'You can count on it,' he replied, and

departed with the air of a man who had done very well for himself.

'Now I can give my attention to you!' Elaine turned her thoughts away from business and looked at Lee. 'What do you think of my place? Is it as good as your father's?'

'I think it's better than Cornwall,' he replied.

'I don't think we should really put your loyalties to the test,' she retorted. 'What would you like to do now? We could set off back to Cornwall today, if you wish. I've finished my business, and there's nothing else to hold me here. Or would you like to stay until tomorrow? I don't know what we could do for the rest of the day, but we could go riding if you'd like. My horse is here, and I'm sure we could find something suitable for you to ride.'

'Let's stay here until tomorrow,' he suggested. 'I don't want to go home yet.'

'You'll have to face your father some time,' she said with a laugh. 'But don't worry about it. He said he wouldn't punish you, Lee.'

'I don't care now I know you're going to stay with us,' Lee replied seriously, and his genuine relief sent a pang through Elaine.

They went riding. She found him a hard hat that fitted and selected a suitable pony for him. Then she saddled her own horse and they set out. It was pleasant to canter over familiar ground, but she was aware that her time here was coming to an end. The future was stretching out ahead, and it intrigued her. She glanced at Lee, and his expression showed that he was thoroughly enjoying himself. But she could not wait to get back to Cornwall. Already she was missing Adrian, wanted to see him again and hear his voice.

A thought struck her as they were riding. She would have to do something about a permanent home in Cornwall! She could not go on living at the hotel. But everything hinged upon Carrie's attitude when they finally met, and for a time she day-dreamed about her mother.

When they returned to the farm, Shaun was waiting in the lounge, and Elaine pursed her lips when Mrs Kemp informed her of his presence.

'I'll take Lee into the kitchen with me,' the housekeeper suggested, holding out a hand to the boy, and he accompanied her willingly.

Elaine entered the lounge and Shaun got up from the settee. He smiled at her.

'Got your business all done?' he asked.

'For the time being, yes.' She nodded.

'May I ask what's going on, or is it all a big secret?'

'Nick and Judith are going to take over here. I'm keeping my interest in the riding school, which Judith will continue to run, and I'm buying a share in a riding school in Cornwall.'

'Does this mean you're leaving this part of the country for good?' His expression closed, eyes filled with a glitter.

'All these changes are being forced upon me,' she replied thoughtfully. 'My life here came naturally to an end with the death of my parents.'

'But they weren't your parents!'

'They were parents to me! But they're gone now and I can't handle the farm and the riding school. My real mother is living in Cornwall, and I have to make a fresh start there!'

'You haven't even seen your mother yet! What if she doesn't want to see you?'

'I'll cross that bridge when I come to it!'

'And what about us?' He eyed her somewhat defensively.

'What about us, Shaun?' She studied his face, her mind troubled. 'There has never been any kind of understanding between us! We were just good friends! Half the time you weren't around, anyway. I've just said that my life here has ended naturally. So I'm going to make a new life for myself elsewhere. That's all there is to it as far as I'm concerned.'

'Will you marry me?'

She suppressed a sigh, then shook her head. 'No, Shaun! I've never been in love with you, and we've never pretended that there was anything between us.'

'You've found someone in Cornwall, is that it?'

'No. That's not true.'

'This lad you've brought home with you. What about his father? Are you interested in him?'

'I haven't been in Cornwall two weeks,' she protested.

'But you're buying a share in his riding school! That's fast work, isn't it?'

'Not at all. I know a good deal when I see one.'

'Things are happening too fast, Elaine! I don't like it at all!'

'I'm slightly dazed myself by the way things are turning out! But it all started with Mother's death. Everything that's happened since is a natural progression of the situation that arose many years ago. I have to find my real mother! I need to make contact with her! And if she is happy to see me then it's only natural that I'll want to live near her.'

'She hasn't bothered with you for years!' He stared out of the window for a moment. 'I'd like to take my holiday now and go to Cornwall with you to see what's going on.'

'No.' She shook her head emphatically. 'I work in an antique shop every morning and at the riding school every afternoon. I don't have any free time at all, so your holiday would be completely wasted. I'm sorry, Shaun, but our paths have diverged, and there's nothing you or I can do about it.'

'I always thought we would get married.' He shook his head. 'I'm in love with you, Elaine!'

'Then I'm very sorry!' She suppressed a sigh. 'I wouldn't want to hurt you for the world, Shaun! I'm sorry if you thought there was a chance we would ever get together. I'm certain there isn't, and it's better for you to accept it now rather than later.

'I'm going to Cornwall to live, returning there tomorrow, and I may never come this way again. Please try to understand my predicament. I've had some nasty shocks over the past weeks and I'm doing the best I can to cope.'

He shook his head slowly, face contorted by an inner pain. Then he sighed and turned away.

'There's not much point in me staying then, is there? You seem to have got your mind made up. Now you have your inheritance you're off, and it doesn't matter about anyone who's left behind!'

'That's not entirely true!' She clasped her hands together, but he stalked to the door and departed without a backward glance. She remained motionless until his car drew away outside.

So that was that! She had severed another tie with the past! She wished it could have been handled differently, but from her point of view there had never been anything between them. She had not considered that he might have been in love with her. He had always been in the background, and never stopped talking about the day she would get her inheritance, even before Mrs Carson had died!

It had always been in the back of her mind that he was interested only in the money! She sighed and pushed the thoughts of it out of her mind. There were too many other things to think about, and she was certain that in a week or two Shaun would forget all about her!

The rest of the day passed quietly. She had Lee for company, and they relaxed, still tired from the long drive the day before. Elaine was aware that the return trip was looming up, and a strange impatience seized her when she thought of Adrian. They watched TV in the evening, and then Elaine nudged Lee and asked:

'Would you like to talk to your dad

on the phone? I think we should have called him earlier!'

'I don't want to talk to him!' Lee was adamant. 'I can see him tomorrow.'

Elaine smiled. 'You're not worried about seeing him again, are you?'

He shook his head. 'You won't let him do anything to me!'

'It looks as if you're getting me summed up correctly!' she said. 'Well, I'm going to talk to your dad even if you don't want to.' She got up and went to the phone, dialled the number, 'Hello! Adrian?'

'He's not here.' It was Margaret. 'Can I take a message?'

'No message, thanks.' Elaine raised her eyebrows. Margaret evidently did not recognise her voice.

'Was it Dad?' Lee asked as she hung up.

'No.' Elaine hunched her shoulders and pulled a face. 'It was Aunt Margaret!'

'You don't like her either!' Lee chuckled.

'I don't dislike her, Lee,' Elaine said seriously. 'I don't really know how she's been treating you, but I do know that she's been good enough to take care of your dad since your mother died.'

He nodded silently, his eyes bright and watchful.

'I would like to know exactly how she has been treating you,' Elaine went on.

'I don't know what you mean!' He shrugged, his expression tense.

'Has she ever hit you?'

'Not hard slaps! But she sometimes pulls me by the arms, and hurts my fingers when she gets angry. She always gets angry when Dad won't do what she wants.'

Elaine shook her head, aware that it was difficult to get at the truth. But she did not think Margaret was ill-treating him! It was more likely that Lee resented her because she had taken the place of his mother. He was still very young, and at his age the loss of his mother was traumatic.

'Exactly why did you hide in my car,

Lee?' she asked. 'I'm only asking because I'd like to know what was in your mind when you did it.'

'I heard Aunt Margaret shouting at you like she shouts at me, and I thought you'd leave and never come back. I hid in your car because I hoped that if I got here with you I wouldn't be sent back home.'

'But you would miss your dad, wouldn't you, if you stayed away?'

'I'd miss you more!' He stared at her with intent gaze, and she smiled.

'Poor Lee! Don't get upset! I'm not getting at you at all! I just want to find out what's in your mind. You know now that I'm staying in Cornwall when we get back. So there's nothing to worry about.'

'I'm not worried now,' he said firmly, and she let it go at that.

Next morning, after breakfast, Elaine put her case in the car and prepared to drive back to Cornwall. But first she called Adrian, and the sound of his voice was like music in her ears.

'Hello,' he said. 'I've been wondering how you were getting along. Has Lee behaved himself?'

'Perfectly. I called last evening but you were out. Margaret answered, and I didn't tell her it was me calling.'

'You don't get along too well with her, do you?'

'What makes you say that?' she countered,

He chuckled. 'Poor Margaret! It seems that she can't please anyone!'

'Well, I've called to let you know that we're on the point of leaving. You can expect to see us about the middle of the afternoon.'

'I'll be looking for you. Give my love to Lee. And be careful on the road.'

'See you later,' she responded, and rang off.

The drive back to Cornwall proved to be uneventful. They stopped at a motorway restaurant for a meal, and Elaine found Lee quite good company. On the latter stages of the journey he began to relax completely, and at times they were laughing and joking. They crossed the Tamar bridge into Cornwall, and sang together. Elaine had never seen Lee so relaxed, and hoped that her company over the week-end was responsible for him becoming less inhibited.

'There we are!' she said at length, when the riding school came in sight. 'Home again! And I bet you wish you'd stayed here all the time, don't you?'

'No, I don't!' He shrugged. 'I wouldn't care if we'd never come back. We could have lived on your farm.'

She smiled and brought the car to a halt in front of the house, and Michaela appeared from nowhere to come rushing to the car.

'Hello,' she yelled, beaming with pleasure. 'You could have taken me with you as well! It wasn't fair that Lee went and I had to stay behind.'

'I had a smashing time,' Lee informed her gleefully as he got out of the car. 'I'm sorry we had to come back.'

Adrian appeared, and Lee pushed in

154

close beside Elaine and took hold of her hand.

'I'm glad to see you back,' Adrian said to Lee. 'But I think you should know you gave everyone a terrible fright. Don't ever do that again. In fact if Elaine hadn't persuaded me otherwise I'd punish you now.

Seeing Lee's fearful expression, Adrian relaxed into a smile. 'Don't worry, Lee, I've said my piece.' He ruffled the boy's hair.

'And I want to tell you something before you go off with Michaela. Aunt Margaret is leaving us at the end of the month. She'll be going back to London to live.'

For a moment there was silence, and Elaine caught her breath. She stared at Adrian but his face was composed, expressionless.

She could see Lee's face from a corner of her eye, and he was aghast at the news, mouth open, breathing restrained in shock. Then he was galvanised into action again, and gulped and looked up at his father.

'Is that true?' he asked. 'You're not just saying that, are you?'

'It's the truth!' Adrian spoke tersely, his face suddenly grim. 'But don't go to her and show her how happy you are at the news. Go and play with Michaela, and don't get into mischief. I want to talk to Elaine before she leaves.'

The two children ran off, chattering excitedly, but Elaine felt cold inside. The news of Margaret leaving had shocked her, and she wondered if her presence had had anything to do with the decision.

But she knew in her heart that it could not be so. Adrian was his own man! He would take care of his own affairs! Evidently matters in the household had come to a head, and the business was being resolved. But she was not entirely convinced by her own thinking . . .

8

'Don't think that Margaret's departure has anything to do with Lee's accusation of ill-treatment,' Adrian said as they walked towards the house. 'It's just a coincidence that this came up the same week-end. I haven't said a thing to Margaret about Lee, except that he was with you.' He lapsed into silence and they walked some distance before Elaine moistened her lips.

'Has it anything to do with me?' she asked, aware that she had to know one way or the other.

'To do with you?' He glanced at her, eyes narrowed, and emotion darted through her breast. 'I don't understand!' He shrugged. 'How could it have anything to do with you?'

Elaine drew a deep breath and explained in part what had occurred between Margaret and herself on

Friday afternoon.

'Perhaps I shouldn't have mentioned it,' she ended. 'But I'd hate to think that I am in any way to blame. Lee overheard some of what she said, and got frightened that I would go home and not come back. That's the real reason he hid in my car. He wanted to make sure I'd keep my promise.'

'I see!' He nodded. 'But it was Margaret's decision to leave. Because Lee was away yesterday, Margaret decided to force the issues between us. She asked me my plans for the future, and suggested that she and I should marry.

'When I turned her down she accused me of being influenced by you, and decided that if there was no hope of marriage between us then she had to leave.'

'Oh, dear!' Elaine shook her head. 'Then I am partly responsible!'

'No.' He was adamant. 'I have never had even the slightest intention of settling down with her! Good Lord! We could never become compatible in a hundred years! But she doesn't see it like that. I'm terribly sorry for her, and we cannot continue as we were. This business would be between us all the time.'

'I'm sorry!' Elaine spread her hands. 'So what happens now? When Margaret goes, I mean! You have Lee to take care of.'

'Hmm, yes.' He nodded. 'That poses a number of problems, doesn't it? It won't be so bad when he's at school, but during the holidays I'll have to arrange something.'

'Perhaps I could help out here,' Elaine said quietly, her thoughts racing. 'I have to find somewhere to live! I can't go on staying at the hotel.'

'And you could live here!' Adrian finished for her. 'Now that sounds like a pretty good idea! We have a Granny flat, did you know? We could clean that up. Then you'd have a place of your own.'

'And when I go into town to the shop I could drop Lee off at school,' she said, 'and be on hand when he comes home in the afternoons!'

Adrian looked at her keenly for a moment, and then sighed and shook his head. 'We'd better pause for a moment and think about this,' he said quietly. 'It's all very well for Lee and me, but what about you? You'd be running this place, and be on hand seven days a week! That's no kind of a life for a young woman!'

'If I don't like it then I'll complain, all right?' she demanded.

'I'm in no position to argue about it,' he replied. 'But I hope you know what you're doing, Elaine. Lee is very attached to you. What would happen if you suddenly decided that you had to leave, perhaps to return to Essex?'

'There's not much chance of that,' she asserted, and he shrugged and shook his head.

'All right, so it looks as if everything is settled. But I don't think it would be a good idea to mention this arrangement until Margaret has gone. If she got to hear of it she might be upset, and she has been very good to Lee and me, no matter what her motives were.'

'I agree!' Elaine nodded, and there was a frown on her face. 'I feel so sorry for Margaret! What will she do when she leaves here, Adrian?'

'I expect she'll go back to London. I'm sorry it had to end this way, but it was inevitable. I must be a prize fool, Elaine, because it never even crossed my mind that she would be expecting me to marry her eventually!'

A car came along the drive and pulled up nearby. Elaine looked round to see Frank Templeton alighting. He came across to them, smiling.

'Hello, Elaine,' he greeted. 'Glad to see you're back safely. Did you have a nice week-end? I must say we're glad to have you back.'

'Yes, thank you, Frank.' Elaine chuckled. 'I had good company all the way.'

'Thank God he was with you.' Frank glanced around. 'My daughter should be here. I have to pick her up a bit earlier than arranged because I'm going out later, and Lorna won't be around to collect her.'

'I'll be here for some time, I expect,' Elaine said. 'I could drive her home later, if it will help. She won't like leaving here any earlier than planned.'

'If you could do that it would help me out of a spot,' Frank said. 'You know, I'm beginning to wonder how we ever managed around here before you arrived, Elaine.'

'It's surprising how she has slotted in and become a part of things,' Adrian agreed, nodding. 'She grows on one, doesn't she?'

'The way Michaela talks about her all the time, it makes me think she's bewitched these children of ours! In a nice way, of course! But, whatever it is, I'll leave you to take Michaela home when she's ready to go, Elaine. And thanks. Mrs Lawson, our housekeeper, will be at home when you get there.'

'That's all right.' Elaine nodded.

'See you at the shop in the morning then!' Frank turned away, and they watched him depart.'

'You must be tired after your long trip,' Adrian remarked. 'Let's go into the house and have some tea, and you can rest, if you need to.'

'I'd rather not go into the house right now,' she protested.

'Because of Margaret?' He shook his head. 'She won't be back until tomorrow morning. She drove into Plymouth this morning. We have a cottage there, and she's gone to think things over.'

They went into the house and Adrian made some tea. Then they sat and chatted, and Adrian began to talk of his hopes and his fears. He wanted to get back to his art, and now he was positive in his attitude. It seemed that he had finally put his grief behind him, and they could all look forward to a bright future.

'We'll smarten up this place now,' he said finally, 'and get some additional horses.'

'I must make some arrangements to bring my horse here,' Elaine observed. 'Perhaps I'll go home again in a couple of weeks to fetch her.'

'And we'll make sure that Lee has not stowed away the next time,' he cut in.

'I'll probably take him along, and Michaela, if her parents will let her go.'

'If I'm asked, I'd come as well,' Adrian said, and Elaine stared at him in some surprise.

'Do you mean that?' she demanded.

'Why should I be the only one left behind?' he demanded, and they both laughed.

'What about this place while we're away?' she asked. 'The horses can't be left alone all week-end.'

'We could take them along as well!' Adrian chuckled, seeming more light-hearted than Elaine had ever seen him. 'Don't worry about them,' he added. 'Tom and his son will stand in for us.'

'Then it's all settled, except for which week-end we'll go. I thought we ought to wait a fortnight at least, so that some of the legal paperwork is finished and we can make it a business as well as a pleasure trip.'

'You're quite a businesswoman,' he retorted. 'I'm certain this partnership is going to flourish.'

They sat talking until Michaela and Lee came looking for them. Lee had given Michaela some lemonade from the fridge.

'Daddy said he was coming for me,' Michaela said. 'It's past six, and he's never late!'

'I'm driving you home!' Elaine explained about Frank.

'Oh good! I can show you round my house.' Michaela clapped her hands. 'Can we go now? If I'm any later I'll have to go to bed before I can show you around.'

Elaine got to her feet. 'I'm ready,' she said, and put an arm around Lee's shoulders when he came to her side. 'I'm sorry the week-end is over, Lee,' she told him. 'I thoroughly enjoyed it.

And we've got some good news to tell you.'

'What's that?' Michaela demanded. 'Are you and Adrian going to get married?'

Elaine smiled, and Adrian lunged at Michaela, caught her and tossed her into the air, catching her and swinging her around before setting her feet on the ground once more.

'You children think you're clever,' he said, winking at Elaine. 'You think you can twist us around your little fingers.'

'Lee certainly can, where I'm concerned,' Elaine said ruefully. 'Anyway, you'd better tell them what the news is or neither of them will be able to sleep tonight.'

'We're going to ask Michaela's parents if she can go away with us for a week-end,' Adrian said. 'To Elaine's home in Essex.'

'When?' Lee and Michaela cried in unison.

'In about two weeks,' Elaine said. 'So you'll have to be extra good until then, because anyone getting a black mark won't be permitted to go.'

'I'll be good,' Lee shouted.

'I'm always good!' Michaela retorted, and stuck out her tongue.

'Come along.' Elaine took hold of Michaela's hand. 'We'd better take you home. And I shan't be sorry to get to the hotel tonight. I'm worn out.'

'And you've got to go to the shop in the morning,' Adrian pointed out. 'Like I said, you're not going to get a moment to yourself this summer.'

'Hard work never harmed anyone!' she retorted.

She drove Michaela home, and the girl invited her in when they arrived. Mrs Lawson, the housekeeper, appeared, and greeted Elaine with great friendliness. But Michaela was agog to show Elaine around, and quickly led her on a tour. Elaine was enamoured by what she saw. The house was spacious and comfortable, and there was an ache in her breast as she looked into her mother's study and saw the place where the Carrie Williams novels were written.

'When Mum gets back I'll have her autograph one of her books for you,' Michaela said. 'You'll like her, Elaine, and I'm sure she'll like you.'

'You're very lucky to have such a famous woman for your mother,' Elaine said, and Michaela shrugged.

'I wish I had a sister like you!' the girl retorted. 'You're such good fun! Lorna is never like that.'

'She has her own life to lead,' Elaine pointed out. 'Now I must be going, Michaela. You can come to the front door and wave goodbye. No doubt I'll see you tomorrow.'

'I'll come to the stable as soon as I get out of school,' the girl promised.

They parted at the front door and Elaine drove into town. By the time she had lugged her case up to her room she was exhausted. She showered, and then sat down wearily, thinking that an early night would not come amiss . . .

Next morning she was at the shop before nine, and waited until Frank arrived. He had to go into Plymouth to examine some antiques, and told her to lock the shop and put the key through the letterbox when she left at one o'clock. Then he departed. She began to occupy her time by cleaning some of the objects, and the morning passed without incident. Later, when the telephone rang, she went to the desk and picked up the receiver.

'Templeton's Antiques,' she said.

'Hello!' A woman's voice spoke in her ear. 'Is my husband there, please?'

Elaine froze. It was Carrie Williams! Her mother! She tried to control the sudden fast beating of her heart, and gulped at the lump which came to her throat.

'I'm sorry,' she said. 'Mr Templeton had to go into Plymouth this morning, and I have no idea when he'll be back.'

'Oh, dear! Well perhaps you'd tell him I called, would you? I'll have to ring again later.'

'Certainly. And if I don't see him I'll leave a note on his desk.'

'Thank you! Frank told me he has employed a capable assistant for the summer. Your name is Elaine, isn't it?' Carrie paused for Elaine to confirm it. 'I do hope you're settling in well. Goodbye now.'

'Goodbye!' Elaine grasped the receiver and held it tightly to her ear. She heard the line cut off, and a sigh escaped her.

It was the first time she had ever heard her mother's voice! A pang seemed to tear her heart in two. She drew a steadying breath and held it for as long as she could.

Carrie would be home soon. Then what? Elaine didn't dare think of the future if her mother didn't welcome her.

She resolutely thrust aside all thought of her mother and locked the shop and departed for the riding school.

'How do you feel after your hectic week-end?' Adrian asked.

'I'm fine, thanks,' she replied. 'I'm certainly glad that I came to this part of the world.' She watched him as she

170

spoke, and the knowledge that she loved him bubbled up in her breast. If Carrie didn't want to acknowledge her as a daughter there was Adrian. And yet, looking at him she saw nothing in his manner to suggest that he had even the faintest interest in her.

'It hasn't taken you long to settle down,' he observed. 'Isn't this your third week here?'

She nodded, wishing she could tell him her prime reason for coming to Cornwall. But Carrie had to be the first she spoke to, she knew, and fought down her impulsiveness. But the growing uncertainty of not knowing how her mother would receive her was becoming nerve-racking.

'Would you like to go for a ride?' he asked, and she realised that he was watching her closely.

'There must be some work to do,' she countered.

'Riding exercise for Juno is first on the list,' he retorted.

'I can't argue with that!' She

chuckled as they turned to the stable.

'I've already saddled the horses,' he told her. 'I must be back around three, so we'd better get moving.'

'I'll just pop into the office and change into my riding clothes,' she replied, pausing in the yard.

'I'll get the horses.' He continued, and Elaine went on to the house.

She heard Margaret moving around in the kitchen, and frowned as she hurriedly changed. But the woman did not appear, and Elaine sighed with relief as she hurried towards the stable, where Adrian was waiting for her. They mounted and rode around the back of the stable to the cliff path. Adrian immediately let the stallion have its head, and Elaine spent the next 15 minutes trying to catch up. When he finally eased the big horse, Elaine managed to get abreast of him, and he laughed when he saw that she was breathless.

'Let's dismount for a few minutes,' he suggested. 'You look as if you could do with a breather.'

Elaine slid out of the saddle and trailed the reins. Adrian came to her side, dropping his reins, and the horses cropped the short turf together. Elaine turned slowly to view her surroundings. They were standing on a knoll overlooking the sea, and she felt dizzy just gazing at all the space that abounded. Adrian moved closer until his shoulder touched hers, and she sensed his nearness and caught her breath as her pulses began to race.

'I've never seen such beautiful scenery,' she observed with a catch in her throat.

'I agree with you!'

There was such a strange note in his voice that she glanced up quickly to discover that he was looking at her and not the scenery. There was a faint smile upon his lips, and his dark eyes were filled with a brightness she instantly recognised. Her heart missed a beat, and suddenly she was emotional and there was a lump in her throat. Tears stung her eyes, and, before she was quite aware of it, they overflowed and streamed down her cheeks. She tried to turn away quickly but he reached out and took her chin in his hand, holding her firmly but gently.

'Elaine!' There was concern in his tone. 'What's wrong!'

'Nothing.' She tried to smile. 'I expect my emotions have been suppressed for too long, and now I'm feeling very happy they're getting out of control.'

'Are you happy now?' He spoke softly.

'Extremely happy! I've made a completely new life for myself, and I don't know where to begin counting my blessings. Just think of the new friends I've got!'

He nodded, still cupping her chin in his hand. 'There's Lee, certainly! Michaela! And there's me, for what it's worth. You've made quite a big impact on me, did you know?'

'Probably because I've prompted you

to make a few decisions on matters you were letting slide,' she suggested.

'You pulled me up short and made me take a good, hard look at myself and life in general! That's when I decided to push the past into the background where it belongs and take life by the scruff of the neck again.' He leaned forward and his nearness sent a tingle through her. Blood was pounding in her temples, and she fancied that he would hear the beating of her heart. 'Lee had the good sense to realise that you were a life-saver sent to help him,' he continued, 'and I'm only now beginning to see that fact for myself! That's exactly what you are, Elaine. A life-saver! Selfless and generous! You've given up most of your summer to help pull us around, and I'm grateful, very grateful!'

His insistent voice seemed to break down an intangible barrier that had stretched across her mind, and emotion rose up inside her. She lowered her gaze, pulled her chin out of his grasp.

The next instant she had pushed her face against his chest. He stood motionless, then slid his arms around her shoulders and cradled her gently. She sighed and closed her eyes as reality fled, leaving her weak and vulnerable. But she could feel his strength, and it seemed to give her the will to face what the future might bring.

9

For what seemed an eternity, Elaine stood huddled in Adrian's arms, and as the timeless seconds passed she slowly rose above the emotion filling her. When she lifted her head to look at him she discovered that he was gazing out to sea, a far-away expression in his dark eyes. He sensed her movement and stirred without releasing her, and when he looked down there was an undefinable sadness in the depths of his gentle eyes.

'You'll be all right!' he said quietly. 'You're such a good person, Elaine!' He lowered his head and his lips touched her mouth. She caught her breath, instinctively responding, and there was such sweetness in their kiss that she wanted it to go on and on. When he eventually lifted his head he still held her, and she gazed up at him, mesmerised by his power. 'I love you, Elaine,' he said quietly. 'I fell in love with you the first moment I saw you! And I'm telling you because I've seen that you've fallen in love with me.'

'You've noticed?' she whispered.

He smiled and nodded. 'Quite easily! You're like an open book.'

'I do love you!' she agreed. 'But I didn't think there could be any chance. There was Margaret! And you seemed so remote.'

'Well, the age of miracles is not past!' He kissed her again and she closed her eyes and relaxed against him. 'One thing we do have on our side is time,' he mused. 'And there's so much to be done. But there's no hurry! I'm just getting over a nightmare, and you've had more than your share of heartache.'

'There is something else in my life!' Elaine realised that she ought to say something about her mother. 'I really can't tell you about it at the moment, but very soon now it should be sorted out, and then I'll break the news to you.'

'That sounds intriguing!' He looked into her eyes. 'I won't ask a single question! But I must say that you've aroused my curiosity.'

'I'd dearly love to tell you about it right now, but it wouldn't be fair of me to divulge details at the moment.'

'That's all right.' He nodded. 'You'll tell me in your own good time, if it's anything I need to know.' He glanced at his watch. 'And I'm afraid we have to be starting back to the stable. I have a business appointment in town.'

Elaine breathed deeply as they rode back the way they had come, and when they had stabled the horses, Adrian took hold of her hands for a moment.

'Elaine, there are some things better kept secret sometimes, and what's happening between us is one of them. It might cause trouble if we reveal our feelings too soon, although I'm ready to shout it from the rooftops.'

'I understand.' She nodded. 'I won't

say a word to anyone until the situation has been resolved.'

He sighed deeply, and she studied his features. He looked into her eyes and grinned.

'You certainly came with the wind of change,' he remarked. 'I feel a different man already. My whole past has fallen into place, and there's no pain now, only relief that it is all behind me. Thank Heaven you decided to come to Cornwall, Elaine.'

She smiled. 'I know exactly what you mean,' she replied. 'Coming here has worked wonders for me.'

He kissed her lightly on the lips and then held her close for a moment. When he drew away he sighed reluctantly, and then glanced at his watch.

'I'm afraid I have to go now,' he commented. 'I'll see you later, at the hotel.'

'I'll be there, and waiting,' she responded. 'It won't matter what time you come.'

He smiled and departed, and she

watched him cross the yard to the house. A sigh escaped her. She felt light-headed, with a feathery sensation in her breast. Her mind was light and cheerful, filled with optimistic thoughts and love. She set to work with new vigour, and sailed through the chores.

'I want a few words with you!' It was more than an hour later when Margaret spoke at Elaine's back.

'What's wrong?' Elaine spun round to face the woman, and leaned on the broom she had been wielding energetically.

'Plenty, it seems.' Margaret came forward a few paces and halted with arms akimbo, her shoulders pushed back and an expression of leering triumph on her face. 'I had a visitor this afternoon while you were out riding with Adrian! His name is Shaun! He told me some things about you! He was going to speak to Adrian about you but I talked him out of it. I think it should be handled more discreetly to avoid upsetting anyone, Lee in particular.'

'Just a moment!' Elaine frowned. 'I don't understand! Was Shaun here this afternoon?'

'That's right. I managed to get him to leave before you and Adrian came back. And I think everyone will be less upset if you disappear without an explanation.'

'Disappear? Why should I?' Elaine's thoughts were whirling. 'Shaun doesn't mean anything to me, and he certainly doesn't have any right to talk to Adrian about me! There's nothing to be said, come to that!'

'Well, you'd better go and talk to him before anything is said!' Margaret's eyes narrowed until they were mere slits. 'I told him the hotel you're staying at, and he's gone there to wait for you.'

'And I have no wish to see him! What on earth is he doing in Cornwall, anyway? He had no right to come here to see me!'

'From the way he was talking I'd say he had every right to be upset. He told me you were supposed to be marrying him in a few months.'

'That's a downright lie!' Elaine gasped.

'Truth or not, how do you think Adrian would take it?' Margaret chuckled harshly. 'If you have any thought at all for him, or the lad, then you'll get away from here as quietly as you can, with no fuss.'

Elaine shook her head, unable to accept that what she was hearing could be true. She walked past Margaret and went out to her car, hoping that Lee was nowhere around. Her mind was in a whirl as she drove to town. She parked, entered the hotel, and paused at the reception desk.

'Is Shaun Appleby registered?' she inquired.

The receptionist checked the register and then nodded. 'Yes. The gentleman is in the room next to yours, Miss Carson.'

'Thank you.' As Elaine turned to the stairs a thread of anger unwound in her mind. Shaun had no right to turn up out of the blue! And what on earth was he saying about her?

She knocked at his door, and after a few moments Shaun opened it and stood looking at her, a thin smile coming to his lips.

'I was just thinking that it was time you showed up,' he commented. 'So Margaret told you I had arrived, did she?'

'She certainly did! And you have no right to talk to people about me. What on earth are you doing here, anyway?'

'I'm on holiday! I have two weeks, and I thought it would be perfect down here right now. It didn't take me long to find out what's going on, either! Margaret couldn't tell me quickly enough!'

'You're making a big mistake, Shaun!' Elaine tried to control her anger. 'You know you have no right to say that we mean something to each other!'

'All is fair in love and war!' he quoted, and chuckled. 'But I'm only thinking of your best interests, Elaine.

You're still emotional about Mrs Carson's death, and the shock of discovering that she was not your real mother must have had a traumatic effect on your mind. I'm trying to save you from yourself, and you'll thank me later, when you've regained your mental balance.'

'There's nothing the matter with my mind!' she retorted. 'And I'm furious with you! Adrian and his family have had enough trouble without you fabricating more! I shall see Adrian myself and explain everything. I won't give in to this! You're trying to blackmail me!'

'And what about your real mother? She's living here somewhere. Who is she?'

'I didn't tell you that, did I?' She smiled.

'You don't have to!' He chuckled. 'There was some talk back home about you being adopted, and the girl who works in the library stopped me in the street yesterday. She mentioned the rumour, and asked if it was true that

Carrie Williams, the novelist, is your real mother. You got all the details about Carrie Williams from the library, and then you came down here. I checked the details myself, and I find that you're even working in the antique shop belonging to Carrie Williams' husband.

'I dropped into the antique shop this afternoon before I went out to the riding school and saw Frank Templeton! He said his wife is away on business, and I've put two and two together and come up with a very promising four!

'My next move is to see Frank again and tell him that you are Carrie's daughter. Just think what a furore that would cause if he doesn't know anything about that!'

Elaine moistened her lips. She did not need to be told the situation. She had gone over it many times in her mind, from every conceivable angle, and she knew that such a disclosure might ruin Carrie's whole life.

'All right,' she said heavily. 'What is it you want me to do?'

'Come home with me! Forget about all these people! They don't mean anything to you!'

'All right,' she said slowly. 'I'll pack and go home! But I'll have to telephone the riding school and explain that something unexpected came up. They'll have to know I'm leaving.'

'Ah!' Shaun grinned. 'You can't catch me like that! I'll do the talking and then I'll know they've got the right message. What's the telephone number?'

Elaine told him, and stood frozen in disbelief as he made the call. The silence in the room seemed to grasp her by the throat, and she pictured Lee and wondered what he would make of all this.

'Hello,' Shaun said. 'Is Adrian there? Yes, it's me, Margaret. I've spoken to Elaine and she's seen the light. She's going home. I'll tell Adrian about it. Is he there?'

Elaine hoped that Adrian was still in

town. With any luck he would not be at home. She uttered a silent prayer, but her hopes were dashed when Shaun continued.

'Hello, yes. It's about Elaine . . . No. You don't know me! I've come unexpectedly from Essex to see Elaine. She has to go home! Some urgent business has come up! No, she can't talk to you! She's too busy packing, and she'll be gone before you can get here. She told me to say that she won't be coming back to Cornwall. She made a mistake about her life here. Yes, I know it's a bit sudden, but that's how it came to her — out of the blue! That's all I can tell you. Goodbye!'

Elaine caught her breath as he hung up. Her heart felt as if it had been squeezed by a cruel hand. He looked at her, and she spoke through clenched teeth.

'Well, you think you've been very clever, don't you? So my chances here are ruined! All right, I'll go back to Essex. But let me tell you this here and now! I never want to see or talk to you again! When you leave me here you walk right out of my life.'

He smiled. 'I expect you to be angry for a time, but you'll get over it, and later you'll even thank me from saving you from all this.' He moved to the door. 'I'll see you when you get home. There's nothing you can do here now. I can always check with Margaret that you have broken all ties there.'

Elaine moved away from him and went to the door of her room, unlocked it while he stood watching, and entered and slammed the door and bolted it. She ran to the telephone, snatched up the receiver and called the riding school. When Margaret replied, Elaine clenched her hand around the receiver until her knuckles whitened.

'I want to talk to Adrian please,' she said curtly.

'I'm sorry but he's just left. He had a phone call a few moments ago and then hurriedly packed a case and left. He said he'd be away for a few days! It won't take him long to get over you, Miss Carson!' Margaret laughed triumphantly, and Elaine dropped the receiver upon its rest as if it had suddenly become too hot to hold.

She began to pack. There was no point in remaining! She would have to stay away until Carrie returned! Then she would put matters right! She fought against utter depression as she took her cases down to the car. She paid her bill and steeled herself to depart. She had actually started to drive out of the hotel car park when it came to her that she had not formally terminated her employment with Frank, and her courage almost failed her as she relocked the car and walking along the street to the antique shop.

Frank was coming to the door of the shop from inside as Elaine opened it to enter, and he stepped outside before she could speak to him.

'Hello, Elaine! I don't usually see you at this time of the day,' he commented. 'Please go in! I won't keep you a moment. I have to run along to the post office before it closes.'

She nodded as he dashed off along the street, and entered the shop and stood near the door, inspecting some of the curios.

'Can I help you?' A woman's voice spoke from the rear of the shop and Elaine turned quickly. The blood drained from her face when she saw Carrie Williams seated at the desk in the little office.

'Oh! I — er, I'm not a customer! I'm Elaine, the new assistant! I spoke to you this morning on the phone! But I thought you were in the States!' She stared at her mother, unable to believe her eyes.

'That's why I was on the phone this morning!' Carrie said with a laugh. 'I was calling from London Airport! My business ended earlier than planned, and I came home as quickly as I could. I wanted Frank to come and collect me from London, but he was in Plymouth. So you're Elaine!' Carrie got up and came forward, extending a hand in greeting.

Elaine felt the touch of her mother's hand and caught her breath. If she could only broach the subject that was closest to her heart!

'I must talk to you,' she said sharply. 'I've been waiting impatiently for you to come home.'

Carrie frowned. 'Is something wrong?' she asked.

'Oh, no! Nothing. I came from Essex to see you, and that's why I took the job here, to be on hand when you returned.'

'I see.' Carrie's frown deepened. 'How can I help you?'

'What I have to tell you will come as a shock, and I don't really know how to start!' Elaine spoke slowly, trying to find the right words, hoping against hope that Frank would not return too soon.

'I'm listening,' Carrie said, her expression relaxing. 'Just tell me what's in your mind.'

'My adoptive mother died a few weeks ago!' Elaine drew a deep breath and moistened her lips. 'After the funeral the family solicitor told me that I had been adopted as a baby. It was the first I knew about it.' She paused, her eyes upon Carrie's face, and she saw a slowly dawning awareness overtaking the frown that had been present. 'The solicitor told me that you are my real mother!'

Carrie moved forward a step and peered intently into Elaine's face, then reached out and took hold of her elbow.

'Can it be possible?' she faltered. 'Are you the daughter I never saw? I can see certain resemblances! You and Lorna! Even Michaela! Elaine! Oh, my dear girl!'

Carrie broke off and threw her arms around Elaine's neck. Elaine was overwhelmed. She closed her eyes and could not prevent tears from squeezing between her lids. It seemed as if her mother might accept her.

'Mother!' she whispered. 'Are you

pleased to see me?'

Carrie drew back and stared searchingly at her. 'Pleased?' She kissed Elaine's cheek. 'If you only knew how many times I've tried to find you over the years! I never saw you when you were born! It had been decided that you would be adopted, and they took you away immediately. Oh, if only I could explain how much I regretted that decision! And you didn't know you were an adopted child?'

'Not until my adoptive mother died! As soon as my solicitor told me I had to come and see you! But I was afraid your husband — Frank — didn't know about me, so I had to see you alone at first.' Elaine caught her breath as fresh emotion assailed her, and she was weeping by the time she had explained the situation.

'You poor child!' There were tears of joy in Carrie's eyes. She embraced Elaine, patted her shoulder consolingly. 'Thank God you have come! And Frank knows all about you! Over the years he's tried to locate you on his travels! A long time ago I gave up hope of ever finding you! And now you turn up out of the blue!'

The shop door opened, the bell ringing stridently. Elaine looked round to see Frank entering, and he paused on the threshold when he saw Carrie with his arms around Elaine.

'What's wrong?' he demanded, coming forward quickly, alarmed by the sight of Elaine in tears.

'Nothing to get concerned about, dear,' Carrie replied. 'Let me introduce you to my daughter Elaine!'

'Elaine! Your daughter?' Shock suffused Frank's face. He stared at Elaine for several moments, and then nodded. 'At last you've found her, Carrie! I can hardly believe it, but I was struck by something about you when we first met, Elaine. Why didn't you say something to me when you arrived and discovered that Carrie was away? I wouldn't have put you to work in the shop!' He slid an arm around Carrie's shoulders, who hugged Elaine. 'This is tremendous!' he exclaimed. 'I'm so happy for the both of you!'

Elaine caught her breath as a sigh quivered through her. She was over-joyed, and could not take her eyes off Carrie.

'I must take you home, Elaine,' Carrie said. 'I can't wait to see Michaela's face when she learns of this! I told her all about you when she was very young, and she's often mentioned you, wondered about you!'

Elaine sighed happily, but deep inside there was a dragging ache because of Adrian, until she realised that she did not have to leave at all! She caught her breath. Shaun's hold over her had vanished the instant she spoke to Carrie. All she had to do now was tell everyone exactly what had happened!

'You two had better go on,' Frank suggested. 'I'll be held up here for a bit. And it looks as if I'll have to find myself another assistant now!'

'No,' Elaine said. 'I'll work the

summer through. I promised.' She paused and then said, 'Would you mind if I went off on my own for an hour? There is something very important that I must do! I'll come to your house when I've sorted it out.'

'Certainly!' Carrie patted her shoulder. 'I'll go home with Frank and we'll see you later.' She leaned forward and kissed Elaine's cheek. 'I'm so very happy to see you! It's my dearest wish come true! Welcome home, Elaine!'

'Thank you, Mother!' Elaine smiled, and felt as if she were walking on air as she left the shop.

She drove out to the riding school, determined to put an end to the mischief that Shaun had created. Just before she reached the turn-off she spotted two small figures on the road ahead. Lee and Michaela were running along the grass verge, and when they saw her car they dived out of sight behind a hedge.

Elaine drew up at the spot, stopped the car and and alighted. She could see

Michaela's red jumper showing through the hedge.

'What are you two doing here?' she called. 'I can see you, Michaela, so it's no use hiding.'

'Elaine!' Lee sprang up at the sound of her voice and came running to her. Michaela appeared at his back, looking sheepish, but smiling because it was Elaine.

'We didn't know it was you or we wouldn't have hidden,' Michaela said. 'We'd only hide from other people.'

'Why?' Elaine looked at Lee, who was sniffing and trying not to cry. He suddenly came forward and threw himself into her arms. She held him tightly as he wept. 'What's happened?' she demanded as she patted his shoulder.

'Margaret has been awful to him again,' Michaela said. 'She told him you'd gone for good and wouldn't be coming back, ever!'

'So we were running away,' Lee said, lifting his head from her shoulder. 'We were going to find Essex and come and live with you.'

'I'm not going away!' Elaine spoke firmly, fighting off her own tears. She held Lee off and looked into his streaky face. 'In any case, you know I wouldn't go away without seeing you first.'

'I told you so!' Michaela declared.

'As for you, young lady!' Elaine said, smiling at the girl. 'There's a big surprise waiting for you at home. I've just come from the shop. Come and get into the car, and after we've taken Lee home we'll go on to your house.'

The children jumped into the back of the car, and Elaine drove on to the stable. As she parked in front of the house, Adrian emerged and walked towards his car. He stopped at the sight of her, and turned and came forward as she ushered the children out of the car.

'Elaine, what are you doing here?' Adrian called as he approached. 'I was just on my way to pick you up at the hotel.' He glanced at the children as they got out of the car. 'Had you forgotten that we had a date this evening? And where did you pick them up? They're supposed to be playing in the paddock.'

Elaine was puzzled by Adrian's calm manner. He was acting as if nothing had happened. She caught her breath as a glimmer of truth began to glow in her mind.

'Adrian,' she demanded, 'have you spoken to someone named Shaun?'

'I don't know anyone named Shaun!' He looked perplexed.

'And you didn't pack a case a short time ago and prepare to go off for a few days?' she persisted.

Adrian shook his head, frowning as he stared at her. He moistened his lips. 'You're talking in riddles,' he complained.

'Perhaps so! But it's all perfectly clear to me now!' Elaine nodded. So Shaun and Margaret had plotted the whole thing! And it had almost succeeded. If Carrie had not come back unexpectedly, she would have gone back to

Essex and that would have been the end of it. She sighed, aware that Adrian was gazing at her, as were the children, all mystified by her questions.

'It's all right,' she said, smiling. 'Everything is all right. I picked Michaela and Lee up on the road. But they're coming with us right now. I told you I had some unfinished business, Adrian. It was all rather a mystery, wasn't it? Well, it isn't any more! There's a big surprise for everyone, and all I'll say about it now is that it's a pleasant one. But before we go any further, I must tell you, Adrian, how much I love you! My heart is bursting with happiness, and I can't contain it any longer!'

She bent and kissed Lee, who clung to her, and then gathered Michaela into her embrace. After hugging them, she stood up and confronted Adrian, who smiled and took her into his arms. There were gasps from the children as they kissed.

Breathless, Elaine broke away from Adrian, her cheeks aflame, eyes shining.

'It's time Michaela went home,' she said. 'Lee can go with us, so both of you hop into the car. Perhaps you'll drive, Adrian, for I'm too excited to trust myself.'

They were all looking mystified as they set out along the road. Elaine glanced around as they left the riding school. She had thought earlier that she would never see it again. But that was now in the past. She glanced at Adrian's profile as he drove towards Michaela's home.

Adrian reached out a hand and grasped her fingers, squeezed them gently. In the back of the car the children were chatting happily. Elaine looked at Adrian and their glances met. There was promise in his eyes! She nodded in silent communication. A weight seemed to lift from her mind. She had found her mother, and a whole new family! And she loved Adrian, was aware that he loved her. She must be the most fortunate woman in the world, she told herself, and realised that it was time to look forward to the future . . .